KEEFIE

KEN CHAMPION

KEEFIE

KEN CHAMPION

First published June 2015

© Ken Champion
The author asserts his moral right to be identified as the author of the work. All rights reserved. No part of this publication may be reproduced, stored in a retrieval system or transmitted in any form or by any means, electronic, mechanical, photocopying, recording or otherwise, without the prior permission of the publishers

ISBN 978-1-326-28512-8

Cover: 1940 – photo by Alfredo Panchim

PENNILESS PRESS PUBLICATIONS
Website :www.pennilesspress.co.uk/books

For
Tim, Steve, Toby

By the same author

Fiction

The Dramaturgical Metaphor
Urban Narratives

Poetry

But Black & White is better
Cameo Metro
African Time
Cameo Poly

Urban Narratives

'His realism is enriched with imagination, the most real of all qualities.'
                        Meredith Sue Willis, Hamilton Stone Review (2014)

The Dramaturgical Metaphor

'An existential thriller which sees psychoanalyst James Kent embark on a disturbing European journey, capturing a sense of time and place that transport us to his host locations whilst also slightly dislocating our commonsensical assumptions. Think Jean Paul Sartre reimagining Alastair Maclean.'
                      Chris Connelley, Hastings Independent (2014)

'The author, often with a deep, unspoken tenderness, introduces a protagonist randomly and artfully directing Kundera-esque scenarios across Europe to escape from a damaged ego while searching for an idealised one. This new novel is not only to be admired for style and pace, but to be felt, to be angry at.'
                              Phil Ruthen, Waterloo Press (2014)

CHAPTER 1

It seemed he now had a brother. After all the nudges and winks he'd noticed people give each other when he was with mum rigidly gripping his hand in the street, the knowing looks from aunts and uncles - uncle Reg had said she looked like 'a house with a bow window and a sweet shop underneath' - the 'oohs' and 'aahs,' the 'You're having a little brother or sister, eh? Bet you're excited.' and dad buying a second hand cot and mum's, 'Oh, for Chrissake, Fred, give it here.' as he clumsily made a mess of painting it, he arrived.

It was 1939. He was almost ten years old and standing on the step leading to aunt Con's scullery at the end of her living room and watching the front door opening and his mother coming in holding a bundle in her arms. She walked down the narrow passage with her sister Doll and stood smiling and proud inside the room. People gathered around her, the women 'aah-ing' and clucking, the men laughing while he stood there, the scene seemingly happening at the end of a long hall like the one at school where they had assembly. But there was no one near him here, no one to put an arm around his shoulder and tell him what it meant, what he should feel. He stood there smelling uncle Reg's beer, and cigarette smoke from aunt Flo who his dad always called Florrie and who lived upstairs at home with uncle Harry. She was wearing a pill box hat and cork wedged shoes; he knew that was what they were because mum had said. Someone opened the front door and his father came in.

'Where yer been, Fred?' uncle Tom asked.

'Workin' wasn't I; I knocked off early as it was.'

He went over to his wife, took the bundle from her, smiled down at it and, grinning, looked around at everybody then down again. Keith wanted him to smile at *him*, just look at him. Somebody put a square of Cadbury's chocolate in his hand; it was aunt Clara. He liked her. She had a big red mouth that was always laughing. It was only then that mum came over holding the fluffy blue thing again and showed him what was inside it.

'Here's your brother, Keith.' She looked at him with her eyes gleaming. 'Say hello to him then.'

He looked at it, it was tiny and pink and ugly with big red hands. He said nothing. He didn't know what to say. She went back to the others.

He usually liked coming here because dad would bring his magic lantern and show pictures on a front room wall of Humpty Dumpty and men with long noses carrying baskets full of long noses, and playing Escalado with his relations putting bets on the painted lead horses moving along the vibrating green track stretched across the dining table. Sometimes he'd be allowed to turn the wooden handle which made a clacking noise like the rattles at the speedway and made the horses hit the lines of wooden studs and keep jerking back until they got through them. They had names like Pink Lady, Big Boy and Black Beauty and dad pretended to be a bookie like his dad used to be. He didn't like coming when he had to play upstairs with his cousin Roy and they'd make things out of putty. He'd once made a house and his cousin had pulled the roof off and pushed it into his face. He wanted to hit him, but knew he shouldn't. He also wanted to cry, but if he'd started to do that and dad was there, dad would have told him not to and say, 'Be a brave soldier, son.' so he hadn't. He liked watching the little horses at aunt Gwen's, too, where they would all stand around the piano in the front room and listen to uncle Albert playing it while aunt Gwen sang 'Sally.' in a strange, high voice and he could see people trying not to snigger. But he liked the sound she made.

It was different at aunt Doll's in Elm Park; she was posh and uncle Charlie worked for the Electricity Board. There was a rockery in her front garden with steps leading up to the door with a sailing boat in the glass panel and she called her back room the living room and the scullery the kitchen. There was zigzag wallpaper and on the armchairs were antimacassars. He liked the sound of the word and would sometimes say it to himself. He didn't know what they were for. When they'd go there, aunt Doll would ask if he wanted anything to eat and pronounce all the consonants in her words, and he didn't know what to answer until mum nudged him and whispered, 'Don't ask, don't get,' and he'd say, 'Yes please.' but he could hardly swallow the dry cake she gave him. She called dinner, lunch, and tea, supper.

'Come on Fred. 'Bye, then, see you, Con,' said mum, giving her sister a kiss and carrying his brother to the front door where she put him into the big black pram that she'd left on the garden path and

CHAPTER ONE

which he'd seen glimpses of in their bedroom at home. He followed them out and watched dad drop his fag on the path and tread on it, saying, 'Bye Albert, cheerio Tom, we'll have a drink one evenin'.'

As they started walking away he said, 'I can't abide that Tom, Ruth, never 'ave, never will.'

Keith wondered, if this was so, why dad had said he'd have a drink with him. This meant the pub on the corner of Tilson Street where he'd have to wait outside while dad brought him some penny arrowroot biscuits or crisps. He peeped into the pub sometimes and it was all yellow and foggy and loud laughs and smoking and men saying thing like, ''ere's to you, Ted.' and 'Pull the uvver one, it's got bells on.' and laughing even louder. He sat in the pub garden with dad and mum in the summer and if uncle Charlie was there mum would whisper to dad that it was his round and that he was as good as Charlie. He liked listening to the music from inside, like, 'If you was the only gel in the world.' and a song about a story and a fight for love and glory which came from a picture mum and aunt Con had seen at the Rex. Sometimes she'd take him to the Broadway where aunt Flo and aunt Daisy were usherettes. He liked their big torches and the palm tees at the top of the stairs.

He heard aunt Con's front door slam and looked across at the greengrocers opposite where she used to bet on real horses, though it wasn't allowed, and was always crossing the road to with a purse in one hand and a fag in the other - which he once thought was either glued on or some sort of growth - and coughing. They walked towards home, mum pushing the pram, while he stayed behind his dad who occasionally turned his head to see if he was still there. They walked to the steps at the side of the station. 'What d'ya come this way for?' mum asked. 'We'll have to bump him up the steps now.'

'It's a short cut.'

'It can't be a short cut if it takes longer to pull him up the steps can it.'

From behind he watched dad slowly pulling the pram up, mum by the side of it looking down at the pink thing. They went past the toy factory where his mum worked, once telling him that when Mr. Colman had moved his mustard making from the same building to one in Norwich he had asked her to go with him because she was such a good worker. They passed the grocers where the man in the apron cut cheese with a wire and where he and his mates sometimes bought lemonade and drank it direct from the bottle. He enjoyed this; doing something he wasn't allowed to do at home because it was bad manners. They crossed the road by the chemists where he thought he could smell the TCP his aunt Gwen used to dab on him when they visited her and he grazed himself playing in her garden. Uncle Albert had a Norton motor bike and sidecar he kept at the side of their house by the fence. Last summer he'd been taken to Southend in the sidecar, but had wanted to go instead with cousin Gordon because he didn't trust uncle Albert's driving. He'd told mum, but she'd said, 'Oh, yer silly sod, it'll be alright. We'll see you there, we're riding with Gordon.' and she'd tied her headscarf on, climbed into the sidecar and been driven off with her scarf blowing back behind her and dad on the pillion with his arms around Gordon's waist.

Somebody afterwards said it was intuition, which he felt was some sort of praise, though not knowing its meaning, but he remembered the sidecar tipping over and being thrown out then looking over the edge of a ditch at aunt Gwen lying in it, her face all white. Some people came and pulled her up and after a time she sat on the pillion again while he climbed back in the sidecar with his uncle riding the rest of the way very slowly.

At the Kursaal they'd watched the 'Wall of Death' where the riders came right up to the top of the big metal drum and roared down again. He smelt the Castrol oil like he did at the Hammers speedway track in Prince Regent's Lane where he sometimes went with mum and aunt Con and watched the riders broadside and Colin Watson doing knee scrapers as he went around the outside of the other riders. They stayed the night in a bungalow at Canvey Island on a muddy road that led to the sea wall. He'd never seen the sea before and it was just a long, grey line of water. He was a bit disappointed.

They went up Maude Road and along Harberson, he again wondering where the names came from. He often wondered where names came from. At school on Fridays, in place of the last lesson, there was a 'Brains Trust' where the older boys and girls and some of the teachers answered the younger children's questions. He'd made himself have the courage to stand up and ask where words came from. Looking down at him from the tables at the front of the classroom and waiting for the giggling to stop, one of the teachers said, 'What a silly question, Clements.' and looking around the class asked for a more sensible one.

CHAPTER ONE

Just before their turning was the Jew shop where aunt Gwen sometimes worked, slipping him the occasional packet of Trebor fruit salad or a stick of Spanish wood to suck - he didn't know it was really liquorice - when Ikey wasn't looking. He wasn't sure if that was his real name, dad called all Jews 'Ikeys' or 'yids' or 'four be twos,' especially Issy Bonn, a singer on the wireless who mum liked. Dad used to give her funny looks when she listened to him.

'What d'yer wanna listen to that Jew boy for?' he'd ask.

'That's horrible,' mum would say, 'he's human like the rest of us, he's got feelings, we're all God's children.'

He didn't know what a Jew was. His dad was always calling people funny names, like 'toe rag' and 'bloody Arab.'

They went past the corner house where the Bowhays lived and he and Terry and goggle eyed Kenny played odds and ends against its side wall, flinging the ball at the ha'pennies - pennies if they were flush - to knock outside the paving slab, but no-one ever seemed able to. Mum would shout down the street at him for his tea and he'd run back and go to the kitchen and, if it was a Monday, stir the washing in the boiler with the bleached broom handle while she cooked. Sometimes he'd run out to the park at the top of the street, past the sandpit, round the bandstand then back again in time for his meal. They passed Doris Hill's house and, opposite, skinny Gwen Miller playing hopscotch on the pavement with her sister. Wearing their mother's high heeled shoes and lipstick, they would often pretend to ballroom dance, with Iris taking the man's part and bending Gwen backwards till her head was almost touching the road.

Because he had a new brother he supposed there'd be another party. They'd all kick their legs out sideways and sing, 'Oh, okey cokey, cokey,' and 'put yer left leg in, yer right leg out,' and they'd shout, 'shake it all about,' and the floorboards in the parlour would bounce and the noise wake him up. He would come out of his bedroom into the passage and stand at the doorway and watch. His aunts and uncles would rub his hair and say 'Aah,' and give him pennies or a thrupenny bit which he would take back to his room, put in a drawer and next day give to dad who was saving them for him till he was grown up. The parties he liked best were the New Year ones, where dad rubbed soot from the grate on his face and they would all go out into the street together in a line and everybody would put their hands on the hips of the person in front of them, stick their legs out to the right and left and sing, 'Ay ay ay ay conga, ay ay ay ya conga, lala la la, lala la la.' Other lines of people would come out of the houses and into their line; he felt like he was part of a dancing snake. He liked them; it seemed, for a while, he belonged.

He couldn't imagine aunt Doll and uncle Charlie dancing in the street like they did, nor their son Eric with his horn rimmed glasses and who was going to a college. When he was at their house they would be talking to his mum and she'd be nodding her head at them and saying, 'Really? Well I never.' but mostly just nodding her head up and down as if she understood what they were saying, but she didn't. She'd never ask what something meant. He understood most of the words his relatives were using and felt that Eric knew he did, too, but his parents didn't. He would look at dad trying to sound his aitches, which he never did at home except when Mister Surrey called for his rent, and wanted to blurt out, 'I'm like you, I am, I'm… ' but couldn't get it out and, looking around him at their bookshelves, wanted to tell them how much he liked reading and dad telling him off for it and, once, taking a book from his hands and throwing it on the floor because it irritated him. 'You and yer bloody books,' he'd said. But he couldn't; he just looked up at them, from one to the other, clenching his hands at his sides.

Before they got to the house he saw Bob the coalman's horse and cart turning into the street. He wanted dad to need some coal delivered so he could go down to the cellar, stand on a pile of it, stretch up and watch the daylight streaming in through the grill at the front of the door step and watch Bob's boots coming nearer. The coalhole cover would be lifted and dropped with a clang then he'd jump out of the way of the black lumps as they came clattering down and run back up the cellar steps before he got covered in coal dust and mum jawed him. 'I'll pay you,' she'd say; though it didn't mean giving him some money, it meant she'd smack him. He asked dad if they were going to have any coal. He grunted, which meant no.

Just before they went up the path to the front door of number thirty eight, he heard, 'Whoop me old Keefie.' from across the road. It was Frankie Nutt grinning at him and pointing to the pram. 'Wotcha got in there then, a little sister or sumfink?' and hurried, smirking, into his house. Keith felt embarrassed. He could never tell his parents when he was embarrassed nor of some of the things that he knew, because they would think him a bit strange. It was a little like when his father took him to a dentist in Stratford a few years before and pretended it was a music shop because he didn't want him to be

CHAPTER ONE

frightened. Keith asked him why he'd said it was a shop when it was a dentist's.

'Oh, you know where we are do yer? Didn't know you knew yer alphabet.'

His father opened the front door, mum pushing the pram in and going through to the back room while he went out the side door, the one uncle Harry and aunt Flo used when they came downstairs to go to the outside lavatory at the back of the scullery. He banged his fist on the tin bath hanging from the fence separating them from the Barrett's and went to look for Bluey, his tortoise, who he'd named after Bluey Wilkinson the Hammers speedway rider. It was right in the middle of the tiny lawn. He tapped its shell and a head came out and after a while went back in. He did it again then, getting bored, asked mum if he could go out.

'Don't you want to look at yer brother?' He shook his head.

'Go on then.'

He ran across the road to Alfie Herd's house. Alfie had ginger hair and his mum had dust on the rim of her hat. He was twelve and told Keith that he sometimes put a picture of Princess Elizabeth on the lavatory floor and played with himself. When Keith felt brave enough he would join the Bowhays in shouting at him in the street, 'Alfie Herd did a turd behind the kitchen door, a cat came up, licked it up and asked for 'apporth more.' then running away. His mum came to the door and told him her son wasn't in. She was wearing her hat. It still had dust on it.

He knew none of the Bowhays would be home; they'd gone to Clacton for their week's holiday, so he walked back to the station, down the steps and along the road that went uphill and squeezed through the railings to the outfall sewer and walked along the path on top of it towards the gasometers. He looked down at the back of the houses all joined together like theirs and with even smaller gardens, some with chickens in. He was standing as high as the roofs and chimneys, some of them had smoke coming out. Sometimes he'd walk the opposite way to where he usually did and look down at uncle Reg's house and wonder if his cousin Dennis was in bed yet. It wasn't far from where he and Frankie Nutt had climbed onto the iron bridge that the District Line trains ran across and squeezed between the girders and clung to them as a train rushed by only two yards away.

KEEFIE

It was getting dark now so he turned around and hurried home, watching lights go on in windows and wishing he could be behind one of them wrapped up warm and with someone like aunt Clara. He got through the railings, went back along the road, up the station steps again and ran home. He knew mum would be angry with him for staying out so late and she'd jaw him again and probably smack him. He wanted, really, to say something to her, something about lying awake at night in his room looking up at the cracked ceiling and at the net curtains at the window beside his pillow and trying to grasp infinity - he'd learnt the word at school - and whispering 'for ever' over and over again, attempting to find a final 'ever' so he could go to sleep, but mostly to tell her that it was all horrible. He wanted to explain what he felt to her, but didn't know how. She would have looked at him suspiciously and said, 'What is it then? What you going to say?' Perhaps he should play with himself like Alfie, but it was rude and his mother or God would punish him for it. She didn't smack him when he got home, but shouted at him and sent him to bed without his cocoa.

He lay there thinking of his brother and his creased face like a little animal's in the cot beside mum and dad's bed and wanted to ask mum what he should feel; the right feeling, a sort of official one, but thought that it would be silly to go to her and say, 'Mum, what should I feel about my brother?' And if dad heard him he'd say to her, 'What's he on about now?'

He didn't go to sleep saying his 'evers,' instead he wondered if dad was going to take him to the Boleyn to watch West Ham play Arsenal. He'd never been before, but knew they played there. Dad always spoke abut the gunners with respect and would show him the penny programme he'd bought when they last played them with a drawing of a castle and a wall with a tile missing from its top and the names of the players laid out like triangles. They didn't watch any football, but a few days later dad said to him, 's'ppose you're getting fed up with all the fuss about your brother ain't yer?'

He then told him they were going to see an air display at Hendon Aerodrome the next Saturday where he could watch aeroplanes taking off and flying close to the ground. He didn't think his mum would be coming because she didn't like a lot of noise, except speedway, of course. He didn't really like dad taking him out, he'd sooner be with his mates over the park climbing trees or playing footie or tin can Tommy in the road, where one of the boys would

CHAPTER ONE

place a tin in the middle of it, shut his eyes while the others hid in front gardens and then would have to discover someone who was hiding before he could run to the tin and throw it away as far as he could along the road. He'd then hide again while the boy had to get the tin and bring it back to where he'd first placed it. Sometimes, one of the girls, like Doris Hill, would play and he would hide in a garden with her. He enjoyed this.

When he was with his father he always felt that he had to take an interest in whatever he was shown. When they went to London to see the Horse Guards in their red uniforms and huge hats sitting on the horses, he noticed, after the soldiers and animals had gone inside and people were leaving, dad had a serious expression and stood straighter than usual and put his feet down heavily as they walked back to the station. When they went to Petticoat Lane and Houndsditch Warehouse his dad always called people 'guv.' He said that to the postman too, and especially to Mister Surrey when he came round for the rent each week, and he'd also touch his forehead or the cap he sometimes wore and which mum hated him wearing indoors. Mum wanted him to go up the Lane because he got 'bargains.' He didn't mind dad taking him to Peg Leg's though, because he only took him once, the other times he went on his own.

Dad said he should learn to play a musical instrument. He'd bought him a second hand banjo and wanted him to learn to play it like George Formby. It was a house next door to aunt Con's, and Peg Leg was an old soldier from the last war. In its back garden Keith watched him swing his good leg a second after the wooden one, almost upright above his parallel bars, his biceps taking his weight. 'C Major.' he'd shout and the end of his peg would kick back and Keith would duck his head to miss it. He'd then drop onto his only foot and roar 'Move.' and point him inside to make some music in the room with the gas mantles, and ashtrays strapped to the armchair. He tried to tune up and would strum awkwardly and try to sing 'Goodnight Ladies.' On the way home he stayed close to the walls to avoid other kids and pushed his school cap into a pocket and attempted to hide the music case inside his jacket else he be seen as a sissy. As he neared home he imagined he could hear the creak of bars and, perhaps, the scream of shells and wondered if, holding his rifle, Peg Leg had huddled close against the sides of trenches. He only went a few times.

What he liked best was when they went to see the pantos at the Lyceum and watched the Crazy Gang and the sand dances, but mostly Pat Kirkwood, who was called a principal boy. It was obvious, the way she kept slapping her thighs, that she wasn't a boy. He also wondered how the chorus girls could kick their lovely long legs so high and what was at the top of them; it was a sort of silky smooth, misty place.

There was a lot of queuing for tickets at the aerodrome, but when they got in he saw a bi-plane fly low over buildings with corrugated roofs and drop a bomb - he could see it fall - on a wigwam which Red Indians wearing long feathers on their heads and carrying tomahawks like in the films ran out of screeching and yelling war whoops as the tent caught fire. It was a bit scary and reminded him of when he was very little and had been taken to Wembley Stadium to see the speedway World Championship and heard the noise of the bikes and the shouting and cheering. He'd never been amongst so many people before and his dad seemed to purposely make him look down from the dark at the lit track. It scared him and he'd been passed to his mother to stop him screaming. If he cried when he was a little bit older, sometimes she would say, 'If you keep crying I'll give you something to bleedin' cry for.' Aunt Con had stroked his cheek and he'd kept looking at the fag in her mouth, glowing. But it didn't feel like him that his mother held or his aunt was trying to comfort; it was someone else. It was a bit like when they were at Margate and he was about to sit on a deckchair and cousin Dennis had kicked it and it had collapsed under him and the top of his finger, which was gripping the wooden side bits, was chopped off. It looked like the cut radish in their Sunday tea. He remembered staring at the sand, which seemed to be spinning round him, and started to look for his finger tip as if he could somehow find it. On the way home from the air show he felt sorry for the Red Indians and vowed never to go up in an aeroplane.

At breakfast the next morning his mother looked across the table at him and asked if he was still saying his prayers. He didn't want to tell a fib, so nodded to her.

'You sure?'

He looked down at his slice of fried bread and said nothing.

'Well, you should, every night. Do you remember what to say? You start off with, 'Please God,' then ask him to keep us all safe, and that includes your brother.'

CHAPTER ONE

He took a deep breath and nodded again.

'Don't forget then.'

He did sometimes pray, quietly, almost to himself. He would say, 'God bless mummy and daddy and me.' He supposed he would have to add his brother now. He didn't know who God was. He thought that, maybe, he was a magic thing, a thing that floated above the houses, above everything, the trees, mountains, the earth. He thought he could be in the ceiling looking down at him. Mrs. Malcolm knew about God. She explained it all to the other boys and girls with him at the bible class in her front room near aunt Gwen's where mum took him on most Sundays. Dad had wanted him to go to the tabernacle on the High Street next to the Diphtheria Clinic where they vaccinated you and where he had a tooth out and had to bite on a metal cube while they gave him gas and put a mask over his face. He thought they were going to harm him or kill him. Mum hadn't liked the look of the tabernacle building and wanted to see her sister, anyway. There was a coloured picture of Jesus on the wall at Mrs. Malcolm's that he liked. He was tall and tanned and fair haired with a ring of light around his head and was looking down at a Chinese girl standing next to a black boy and white boy. They were looking up at him, his hand on the girl's shoulders.

He would sooner be there than in West Ham Church where he had to sit very still between his parents; if he didn't, dad would dig him in the chest with his elbow and tell him to keep still and call him 'fidget arse.' and mum would probably hiss, 'What, got St. Vitus' dance have yer?'

When they had to pray he would kneel on the red cushion on the floor and dad would press his hand on his shoulder to keep him down as if he might run away. He was frightened of God, really, because people were always telling him that if he was wicked he would be punished by him. Occasionally he wanted to swear like dad did, but thought God might hear him. The week before, he'd heard a boy in his class at school swear and after the lesson had told the teacher what he'd said and the lad was told not to repeat words like that and to wash his mouth out. He saw the boy being told off and felt guilty and disloyal and went home and sat in his room trying to push away the guilt by telling himself that he didn't like him. If the other kids had found out they'd have shouted, 'Tell-tale tit, suck yer mother's tit.' at him. He supposed that God looked like his Headmaster at school; very stern and severe and always looking for someone to cane, though he didn't have a grey beard as, he supposed, God had.

Ruth Clements opened the front door and closed it behind her. She walked through the narrow passage past the cellar door, noticing that one of the brass stair rods needed a bit of a shine and into the back room with the Zebo-blacked range stove and a bronze statuette on the mantelpiece above it. There was a drawing of a horse Keith had done at school next to it. He'd probably put it there himself, but she didn't like his drawings around the house; there was a place for everything. He was always drawing or reading, anyway. She was the only one in; Flo was still at work at Woolworths, Fred was on a late shift and Lenny was at Gwen's who said she'd bring him back by six. She had to admit that she was probably lucky to have a sister like this who would look after a five month old child like she did; it allowed her to go to work and bring in some money. Mind you, Gwen was a bit selfish really, not wanting kids of her own.

She didn't like cleaning the bank in the city, the train fares were a bit steep and some of the toilets, especially the men's, were filthy. She didn't really like men, she supposed, Con's husband Tom was a horrible man. She suspected that his family may have been foreign, but it wasn't that, live and let live, she'd always say, Flo's Harry probably had some foreign blood in him, too, which you'd expect with a name like Milo. It was the way Tom treated Con, always moaning about things like his food, especially if she was late in bringing it to him, and occasionally grumbling because he thought she might be spending too much on her little flutters on the horses. He was a good decorator, though, and had done up the house smashing, with rag rolled panels on the walls and beautifully grained doors. He frightened her a bit, but she'd have a go at him if she thought he'd been ill-treating Con. That was one thing Fred would never do. He'd never laid a finger on her; though she did wish he was more talkative, it was hard to get anything out of him sometimes, especially about his feelings. He was a good provider though; her weekly housekeeping money every Friday on the dot. He was pretty handsome she thought, unlike herself, with her long nose and thin face - though knowing she had nicely shaped shoulders - and nothing like his sisters with their round faces, thick, dark hair and tiny waists. He'd been a bit shy, still was really, and he had a bit of a temper about him, but then, who could blame him with a father

CHAPTER ONE

like he had: cropped grey hair, braces, collarless shirt and thick soled boots. She had once heard him say that all a woman needed to keep her happy was, 'a thick pair o' lips to kiss and a pair o' boots to kick her.' He'd once knocked Nan's teeth out when he was drunk.

Fred liked his rituals; like the Friday night one when she'd bring the bath in, put it in front of the grate and fill it with saucepans of water from the electric geyser for him to soak in for an hour. They would then probably go up 'The Harold,' have a few drinks, she liked Tia Maria, with Flo and Harry usually, never on their own, while Peggy next door sat with Lenny till they got back.

She wasn't sure whether or not she liked being in the house by herself. She looked around her at the net curtains hanging from the middle bar of the small bay window which she'd put there mainly to blot out the sight of the bath, the Barrett's couldn't see over the fence unless they stood on a pair of steps - though she wouldn't have been surprised if Mrs. Barrett's son had - and they stopped Flo and Harry looking in as they passed. She looked behind her at the stove, it needed blacking again. She'd have liked a modern fireplace like Doll's, but then, they were buying their place and look where it was; there were trees in the streets and in the front gardens, too.

She went back down the passage, looked at its lincrusta'd half wall, noticing some chips of paint off here and there, and at the inside of the front door with its small, domed bell and the cable snaking up the door and out through the hole that Fred had taken two hours to do. The skirting boards had taken some knocks too; probably from the pram, and the carpet was showing patches of thread. If they ever left here the carpet would be Surrey's, though she had bought a bit of coconut matting to put behind the door for Fred to stamp his feet on when he shook his raglan if he'd been caught in the rain. He looked so grim when he did that, so deliberate. He was looking more and more like his father. The bedroom was okay, though, but she didn't like the way he put his packet of 'Ona' contraceptives on top of the other things in the top drawer; she didn't want Keith seeing them if he should ever go in there. She preferred Flo's bedroom, it was nice and big and she could look out and see the people walking by below. She'd hold Flo's legs in when she leant out and cleaned the outside of the windows. Sometimes, one of the Thornton girls next door would be cleaning their upstairs windows at the same time and they'd have a bit of a laugh. It was usually their mother who would let her know if it started raining and she'd put her washing out, shouting, 'Rainin,' Ruthy, rainin'.' On occasions it seemed that all the back yards were filled with screeches of 'Rainin,' Dolly' or Annie or Edie and she'd watch their turbaned heads looking as if they were hurrying along the tops of the fences to pluck their sheets and tablecloths off the lines. Well, cleanliness was next to Godliness.

As much as she liked Flo, and not just because she was Fred's sister and she'd miss her if she left, Harry wasn't always easy. Something about his eyes, a bit shifty she sometimes thought, as good looking as he was; that dark, wavy hair and pencil 'tash. Fred's sister Elsie told her once that she thought he looked like Warner Baxter. That as maybe, but she wouldn't like him grabbing hold of her. He was a bit too full of himself for her liking. When he was coming down the stairs and she'd just come out of the parlour it seemed an intrusion, as if he was walking into her home, into her life. When they were having a meal she could see him through the frosted glass panels of the back room door walking past to the side door then, through the nets, see him go by the window. She felt that he shouldn't be there.

She went into the parlour, tweaked one of the curtains and straightened a picture hanging from the picture rail; it was a Constable print, one of Fred's, she never had liked it. Though it had a lot of greenery it was somehow dark and old fashioned. 'You can see every leaf in them trees, every little detail. Now, that's what I call art,' he'd say. She preferred the painting of the sullen looking lady in the back room; there was something she sympathised with, it was her expression, there was a… stoicism. She'd heard Harry say that once in the pub when he thought that she couldn't hear him.

'Your Ruth's a bit of a stoic, Fred.'

She had an image of Flo again; her figure and dark eyes and hair, like hers, but the grey was showing through hers again and she didn't have Flo's bust, nor her legs, her own were skinny. And there was her laugh, everybody seemed to like it. She couldn't laugh like that, people wouldn't expect her to she supposed. Reg used to call her 'mizhog' when they were kids.

She looked at herself in the mirror above the fireplace; she needed a new blouse and a new hair style; fat chance of those at the moment with no overtime at work. She'd ask Flo to do it when her and Harry had had their tea and they'd go into the scullery and have a few laughs. Flo told her a good one the last time she coloured her hair.

CHAPTER ONE

She said Harry and she were in the bedroom and she thought that he didn't look too well, so she asked him what was up. 'If I tell you will you sit on it?' he'd said. He was a bit outrageous sometimes, they both were, really, but they did make her laugh and she preferred the ones Flo told her than the things Max Miller said on the wireless. She supposed most men were like it, really. She remembered when a plumber had to put a new tap in the scullery and Flo had got a bit friendly with him and when he'd finished he looked at Flo, put his toe on the floor and kept sliding his foot forwards and backwards like a rutting stag. It was very suggestive, but she was glad that he'd looked at her as well as Flo when he did it.

Fred would never do anything like that; maybe a few little smirks and grins with Albert and his smutty jokes down the pub - Gwen called him a walking seaside post card - and, with a drink in his hand, sometimes he'd throw his head back and laugh, but as if he was expected to. He rarely laughed with her and meal times always seemed so grim, so silent and, except for the scraping of his knife around his plate catching the remains of his bacon and eggs or dumpling stew, he'd hardly say a word other than to tell Keith not to talk with his mouth full. She'd somehow assumed that nearly all families behaved like this, but had noticed at Doll's how she and Charlie and Eric always talked to each at meal times, discussing things like politics and what Eric was doing at college and perhaps a play they'd seen at the theatre in Hornchurch. She'd never seen a play, though would like to. She'd been to pantos, of course, and enjoyed the occasional outing to the pictures with Keith. A little while ago, when they went to Stratford Broadway to see 'The Wizard of Oz,' Flo and her sister Daisy were standing in the foyer there dressed in usherette uniforms. She couldn't believe it at first, but they'd started part-time a few days before, Flo wanted it to be a surprise. They looked good in their uniforms, especially Flo; she held her torch in a way that made her look so attractive and sexy, somehow. She noticed Keith standing there staring at her She told him not to stare, it was rude.

She put on a pinafore, went out to the lavatory, scrubbed its floor and poured some disinfectant in the toilet bowl before deciding she may as well do the front step while she was at it. She went back through the house, washed her hands then went into the bedroom and looked in the wardrobe. Other than Fred's suit and shirts and some dresses and skirts of hers, there wasn't much there, but she was fond of her new coral pink woollen jacket which, when out with Flo, she liked wearing with her black slacks. She didn't dress up often; there didn't seem anywhere or anyone to dress up for, except the pub, the pictures and going to the seaside. She rarely felt like dressing up for Fred; he'd probably never notice and as much as she liked wearing lipstick she knew that he'd think she looked like a tart; he hated the smell of nail polish, too. It was different between Flo and Harry; she nearly always had lipstick and eye make up on and Harry seemed to like it, she could tell by the way he looked at her.

She sat on the edge of the bed thinking about her husband. He was so set in his ways: when he came in from work and it had been raining she knew exactly the time gap between the sound of the key in the lock and the shoe stamping starting on the coconut mat, and he was always telling her what he was going to do in the house and when he was going to do it. 'Just going down to get some nails,' he'd say, and she'd picture him in the cellar with his torch looking for the nail jar on the shelves Harry had put up for him, or 'Just gonna wind this clock up, noticed it was a bit slow 'smornin'.' and when she asked him what he wanted in his sandwiches for his shifts at work it was nearly always, 'a coupla slices o' bread and drip.' It was the same in bed after the pub on Fridays, she knew exactly when and where he would touch her, and then he didn't do it properly. It was crash, bang, thank you ma'am and it was finished. They called it 'foreplay' now, but there was none of that. He always grunted twice before he rolled over, his back to her; one loud and one soft. Sometimes, under her breath, she mimicked the same noises at the same time as his. She used to say goodnight to him afterwards, but not now.

When they'd first met, she'd been walking along Stratford High Street after popping in to see a friend who lived nearby when a dog had barked at her as she crossed a side street. It was a greyhound on a leash, at the other end of which was a man about her height with dark hair, grey eyes and a surprised expression. He'd pulled the animal back and apologised to her. He seemed a decent man. He asked her if she'd go to the pictures with him. They saw 'The Desert Song.' the next evening. She was then living in Bow with her mum and elder sisters while he lived with his parents and four sisters in a small terrace house off Plashet Road. When she first met his parents she came away with two strong impressions. One was that she instantly disliked his father, with his braces and boots and his

CHAPTER ONE

grunting most of the time - she thought perhaps that was why she'd refused Keith when he asked if he could have a pair of boots like some of the boys at school - the other was an instant feeling of envy. This wasn't because he had a father; never knowing her own, and her siblings, mother and herself living in a workhouse for a year in Stepney, but how attractive his sisters were, especially Flo and Rose; 'curvy' was the word she used. They also had big, white smiles.

She was six months pregnant with Keith when they married and lived in lodgings in East Ham. Nobody said much about the situation, though she was convinced that the general opinion was that they'd had to get married. She was almost sure she would have done, anyway. The dog he'd had wasn't a racing greyhound, but now he had one that was trained at Romford Stadium. It didn't run much and never won, but she sometimes thought that he was more interested in the animal than in her. She felt a tear. She sniffed and went through to the scullery and made herself a tea.

CHAPTER 2

"Spring is sprung, da grass is riz, I wonder where da boidies is.'
'Da boids? Da boids is on da wing.'
'Dat's funny, I always tort da wing was on da boid."
'D'ya hear that? Dey takin' the mick out of our accent?'
'Not me, that's you, Billy.'
'Yeh, you're the posh one alright, Rob, all da words.'

It was September, 1935, and Robert Costain was in a burlesque theatre on 42nd Street with friend and fellow chippy from a job they were working on two blocks away at 47th and Lexington. The second fittings they were doing had been a 'job and home' so they'd gone for a pleasurable hour or two to see Abbott and Costello at 'The Palace.' He knew that he spoke a little differently from the other guys on the job; he'd been told the same at Tech. School and his father occasionally called him 'Posh Bronx,' Robert feeling the label was one of rejection rather than admiration. Though he wasn't aware of any deliberate reconstruction of that part of himself it could have started from way back; reading things as a child that revealed to him worlds other than his own; of language, values and attitudes. They left the theatre and got the Subway home where he continued thinking of how he'd answer his first social psychology essay set by the lecturer at his new college. It both excited and scared him. A few years had passed since his old school and his A grades, despite which his father's, 'Get a trade behind yer' advice had cemented a cultural inevitability and he'd landed up as a cabinet maker, now working on the Chrysler Building in East Manhattan.

He'd been there for two months and it made a change from most of his jobs in the older buildings of the city where he'd done some skilled carpentry, often referred to as 'East Side' work, but had never earned his living so high up as in this building. The work wasn't as detailed as he'd been used to and he was trying to adapt to these new styles and designs. He was more familiar with the colonial style of panelled doors, elaborate architraves and skirting boards, the occasional Spanish modes and the Georgian. The interior work in this current fashion was less ornate, with chevrons and ziggurats replacing scrolls and gables, more brightly decorative and, a recent word he'd heard, 'streamlined.'

CHAPTER TWO

When he first came to this job he'd looked across to the Empire State a mile away and was reminded of a photo that Jake, the owner of he and Jess's favourite neighbourhood bar in Wilder Avenue, had put up of some guys sitting calmly on a girder eating their lunch. It fascinated him, it was almost as if they were sitting in the bleachers waiting for a game to start; the one on the end of the girder cadging a light from his buddy, another peeking at a workmate's lunch; the cloth caps, the boots, East River beyond, Manhattan below. Maybe, he thought, the next day the man at the side of the cable would be playing pool with the boys downtown and the hatless one be with his dark haired Sue at Coney Island, elbows jutting in *contrapposte* burlesque, giggling into a Kodak, while the rest of them went to a diner or a fight at Madison. Then it was back to the metal and chains, the rivets, the heaving, and the grappling with memories they couldn't hold, which floated away, snatched by the high wind below the steel.

On the evenings Robert went to his class he would leave early, not telling his gang where he was going, except Billy. What thrilled him about the subject, though he wouldn't have been able to articulate it if asked, was that, because of the detachment it seemed to need, it justified his own, often jarring, distance from the values and mindsets that had swirled around him all his life and which he could now categorise and give names to, turn them into social facts, analyse them, dissect them from a distance, and validate his relative alienation from them. His thinking, through many of his experiences, was now a legitimate exercise, his detachment academicised and would be more so if he got to university.

'Yer don't wanna expect no free ride,' Billy had told him. 'It's not as if you're some kind o' rich New Hampshire guy or somethin' that can afford it easy. If you wanna go you gotta pay the fees. I still don't understand why you're doin' it, yer gettin' good dough here, we were lucky; we went through all this time without gettin' laid off. But yer gotta do whatcha gotta do, I guess.'

It was similar to his father, who he'd taken for a beer and who had told two strangers in the bar what his son wanted to do.

'Bet yer proud of him, uh?' one of them had asked.

'I woulda been if he'd got there at eighteen, and anyway, he's bringin' in good money each week, plenty of overtime, his wife's earnin' steady, what's he wanna go for?'

He wanted to shout that with a father like him he it was a wonder he'd learnt to crawl, but knew that was unfair, he, too, was a product of his environment, but, for Robert, his parent seemed at times to be just an unquestioning, unthinking reflex. He knew he couldn't explain to him that to work all the hours God sent to get a decent wage shouldn't be perceived as a privilege, a bonus, a generous concession by the owners of factories and labour. His father had once told him in his teens that he didn't want a communist in his house and had threatened to throw him out of it, neither really knowing what, exactly, a communist was. He didn't want to be handling a saw and spitting out nails for ever, he needed to use his brain and share it with others and he'd been saving hard for the experience. Jess, after some persuasion, seemed quite happy to go; she was in a rut as a switchboard operator and clerk and liked the idea of new people around her, new happenings.

He needed two subjects to qualify so chose, on a different night, to do Literature. The teacher was conservative and uninspiring, but Robert balanced what he had to study by reading Hellman and writers from the Vanguard Press. He'd recently found a copy of 'The Ragged Trousered Philanthropist' in a European bookshop on 59th Street, but knew he could never convince his workmates of the validity of its writer's views; their bias against any form of socialism a part of the constructed consensus of the American psyche. They would probably respond in a similar vein as they recently had when he'd started to explain the concept of consciousness. 'Rob,' said one of them, 'you'll vanish up yer own ass one o' these days.'

The beginning of his university experience at Union Reisler in Brooklyn a year later was initially a struggle. Other than for his recently completed entry subjects he had rarely put pen to paper except compiling crosswords with a friend, producing scattered pieces of mundane poetry and filling in time sheets on the construction sites he'd worked on for most of the preceding fifteen years. Such had been his environment during this time he would have been justified, he thought, in thinking that Higher Levels were probably newly introduced implements to measure the horizontal exactitude of ceilings. Jess had got herself a clerking job in the admin section which helped pay the rent for a small apartment a mile away from the university. He'd suggested several times that she do a course somewhere herself; she had, at one time, been a temporary

CHAPTER TWO

classroom assistant at a Junior school in the Bronx, being verbally abused on a few occasions, though not telling him at the time in case he'd marched straight up to the school. It was a Catholic establishment and he wasn't sorry she'd left it, though it made little difference to the ritualised enthusiasm of her Sunday churchgoing, a subject they'd chosen not to discuss.

He'd first met her when on holiday in Seattle with Billy. He'd never been outside of New York State before, he'd been to Albany and Lyons Falls at one time, but Pelham Bay Park, the Zoo and Long Island usually marked his boundaries. They'd got the light rail to Downtown Seattle and wandered around Central Market and through the small square under the rooftop cantina with its samba band, hip-swaying Mexican Seattleites, and the creaking arses of the English and European tourists just missing the beat. It felt like a different country sometimes; softer and slower accents, food he found difficult to conceptually validate, like curry and mushroom croissant, marinated pecans and balsamic reduction, and Mexican waiters repeatedly asking if they wanted their food boxed.

They'd taken the ferry to Bainbridge Island because they liked the trips to Staten Island they'd been making since their early teens, and this one, too, was like a mini-cruise with the city dwindling away at the stern, but here with a mountain range ahead of them, not an island. She was on her own, holding onto the deck rail, looking down into the water, frowning and very still. He saw only her profile before she turned as if sensing someone looking at her and smiled at him. He'd taken a deep breath and gone over to her, leaving Billy frowning at his back. He discovered that she'd been visiting an aunt who she hadn't seen since a child and who had invited her to stay with her family in Seattle and was returning home the next day. When Robert realised that she lived only a few blocks from him in the Bronx his friend may as well have been on his own for the next few hours. As they got off the ferry Billy had pointed out the clapboard houses with pine trees and maples in their gardens, the automatically sprinkled lawns and Chevrolets and Cadillacs in front of double garages. This was a world away from the urban aesthetic of home. Robert had responded vaguely, mostly nodding absently at his friend's comments. He wrote to her the next day. He and Jess had married less than a year later.

He liked the feel of this campus, as he had when being interviewed there two months before by a fat, sympathetic man who tended to laugh a lot at jokes that Robert had first heard at eighteen, not realising that academics tended to tell the same jokes to fresh intakes each year. He wandered about the neat, almost French looking lawns and gardens watching tall girls walking around in twos and threes talking and laughing with each other in their blouses and belted waists or shoulder padded jackets and skirts worn just below the knee. He felt an excitement; he'd never known women like this, had rarely spoken to them except when doing some work for them; repairing an antique chair, perhaps, or making a sideboard. The scene made him want to buy Jess a decent outfit; he would when he could afford it.

He'd decided to Major in the subject he'd first been introduced to a year previously and plunged into it almost aggressively, spending hours in the library and occasionally at the beginning gently plagiarising until becoming more familiar with the style of writing required. His momentum was halted somewhat when he was required in the first term to do some anthropology and economics. He couldn't relate to the *ceteris paribus* of the latter and as he wasn't very good on family structure, not really sure who his second cousin was let alone working out the complex familial relationships of the Ukuni tribe, had compensated by having a fellow student, Mick, a births, deaths and marriages reporter for a local rag, write his anthropology essays and he completing the other's sociology ones.

As well as Mick, there were other mature students he became friendly with: Guy, a Berkeley reject who had no intention of working and would, perversely, rather get a Fail than a poor *Cum Laude*, figuring it would carry more status, and an ex military pilot who had tipped his Curtiss Falcon straight over the side of his carrier into the Pacific and decided to run away to college. Somewhere he'd picked up a blonde Norwegian for a wife and, following the quickly accepted norm of mutual entertaining between married student couples, they were greeted when being fed at his home, an ample house just outside the city, by lit wooden torches in the garden forming a flare path to the front door. And there was Blind Bob, cruelly nicknamed because of his failing eyesight, doing a Masters in Art History and living in a newly built moderne block of apartments on the campus for married students, who seemed obsessed with painting bus passengers at various stages of climbing the stairs to the upper deck. Jess seemed to like their get-togethers and, though she wasn't awed by his colleagues, Robert could see those slight

CHAPTER TWO

hesitations and rather too late interest when, asked what she did, she answered that she was a clerk, but she 'read a bit.'

He was happiest when, after a particularly stimulating lecture, he'd join the others in the student coffee bar, discussing what it had really meant, what essay titles to choose, debating, arguing, knowing he should have been with these people in this place years before. Though sometimes feeling an undertow of dislike for some of them he was aware that it was envy of backgrounds that gave them an unthinking sense of entitlement, especially the younger ones, some of whom sporadically wore blue overalls to denote that they were on the side of the workers in this time of large scale unemployment. But, as he got to know them he began to warm to them, even Guy with his perpetual sneer, and his girl, Amber, who had come with him from Berkeley, never mentioning why they'd both left. When they'd received their first term assessments Guy told him he thought Robert was a con artist.

'You with your Bronx talk, getting marks like that, eh?'

He'd said it jocularly, but there was, mixed with the surprise, a hint of patronage. And there was Zeta, with her clipped, almost English accent and who'd studied at the Laboratory Theatre, surreptitiously sharing Guy's surprise.

It went on: the essays, the learning, debating, the hours in the library, the student bar; sometimes he didn't want to go home even when there was no reason to stay. He saw the Upper Manhattan girls strolling elegantly around triggering Hollywood created fantasy images, some of which, barely aware of their origin, he'd pushed unsuccessfully onto Jess. She was five feet three and wore her hair short and he had insisted she grow it long and wear high heels. She had complied for a while before returning to herself; a triumph of substance over image.

One evening over supper he remarked on the growing habit of eating hot food on the Subway and that it was capitalism rampant.

'I want it all and I want it now, it's a kind of solipsism, Jess, the philosophy that only self exists. It seems to be mostly women; I don't want to be accused of vulgarised inductive thinking, but, they sit down, root in their bags and out come the crisps or - '

'I'm not interested in your dislikes or theories, Rob, nor in vulgarised inductive thinking, either, talk to your pals about it.' She'd got up from the table and told him she was going out with a friend.

'We'll probably see a movie.'

She hadn't behaved like this before. She got back late. He pretended, not analysing why, to be asleep.

It was towards the end of the first year when a new lecturer arrived from England. The only things his class knew of him was that he'd graduated from Kings College, London and his name was Norman Lee. There was a mild air of expectancy in the smaller of the lecture theaters he first walked into looking rather pugnacious and who, Robert guessed, was about ten years older than him. He had no notes and used the lectern for leaning on. He wrote his name and that of the subject on the board, turned slowly to his audience and said casually, 'Incidentally, God didn't create us, we created God.'

There were frowns, some head shaking, a few giggles, a quiet but audible gasp from a catholic adherent and some nods of agreement.

'I say that not to offend anyone's upbringing, their primary conditioning, but to emphasise that if your head is full, or perhaps, partly full of religious belief, then it will be even more difficult for you to rid yourself of judgements while we attempt to look at the objects of knowledge we are studying with as little bias as we possibly can. Perhaps with some of the views and theories we'll talk about you'll feel disgust; outrage even. Push that away and think, intuit, empathise if you can, and before someone says, 'That's not scientific.' science isn't either; science is a self contained conceptual system, a belief system that of itself can be neither right nor wrong. The same, of course, for maths or, as you tend to say, 'math;' as symmetrically and logically beautiful its interior it doesn't tell us anything of the existence of things. I also don't want to be able to accuse you of making general inferences from particular instances; that is, policeman O'Driscoll having big feet doesn't mean all New York policemen have big feet.'

Robert raised his hand. He felt a little nervous until realising that it was merely because of the man's accent triggering distant and virtually unconscious echoes of his country's colonial past. He asked if he was telling them not to generalize because psychology itself was a generalizing enterprise; the Oedipal, manic-depressive, etcetera. His lecturer smiled.

'No, I'm telling you not to make assumptions based on limited experience; but you're quite right of course that we make generalizations. If we're going to theorise we have to, do we not?

CHAPTER TWO

Each individual for us is a particular case of general law or, rather, a theoretical position. And let's not be as outraged as the Viennese middle classes were when Freud proposed that a child's sexuality begins pretty soon after his birth; try to rid yourselves of morality for a second.' He looked at them seriously. 'Personally, I don't think Sigmund goes far enough; not just that he didn't emphasise birth experience or, indeed, say much about the womb, but the idea that a baby may actually want his father to take him over, to dominate him, if you like, and,' he paused, 'you won't like this; to fuck him.'

He looked around the class. 'I can see the shock on most of your faces, though I think that underneath it there may be consideration beginning. But don't confuse what I suggest a baby feels with what a baby thinks; babies don't, they can't, they have vague pictures in their heads. Another question raised here, of course, is whether there can be thought without language.'

Robert felt that frisson again, just as he had in his first evening class which now seemed such a long while ago.

'Okay, we'll talk about this another time. Let's begin with stereotypes; what are they for?'

Again Robert was the first. 'Because we search for order, society gives us them; man as essentially insecure'

'Yes, it seems so; isn't the hijab a manifestation of that, men covering up the bodies of their women because they're sexually insecure? That's just one learnt manifestation; any more, anyone?'

So it went on, and all a thousand miles away from Billy and the construction sites they'd worked on for so long.

During the Fall term of his second year he was again in Lee's seminar group, having spent the summer, because he and Jess had had to leave their temporary home to make way for the next batch of married students, in a mobile home in a car park to the north of the university. They'd often used the nearby picture houses and cheap cafes to escape from its claustrophobic cramping before finding an apartment in a rundown tenement block that was being refurbished by the university. He'd still gone to the campus, mostly to read in preparation for the next term and to see fellow students who hadn't gone home for the vacation. He also did some carpentry for some people he'd got to know a little; one of the janitors, a cook in the refectory and two lecturers living in Riverdale, and occasionally meeting Jess for lunch when she could get away from her job. He enjoyed the group again, though Lee, busy with lectures and research, often had one of the other teachers fill in for him; the seminars not being the same without him.

He spent the next summer break doing the same. For one of the teachers he repaired the decking of the wraparound veranda of his house and for another made a headboard and mended some chairs. He charged reasonable prices, especially the lecturers; being glad he'd done so when, during Finals, one of them had, because of Robert's almost ineligible scrawl, shown two of his papers to a typist to try to decipher for him. Fortunately she'd succeeded.

In a classroom just before the mid term break, Norman Lee told them he'd come to this country mostly because of the new things that seemed to be happening in psychiatric theory and that he'd spent a few months as an intern in a mental hospital in London. It was an old Victorian building with the end of one of the wards just twelve feet away from trains thundering past.

'There was that sweet anaesthetic smell that gluts the nostrils, the disinfectant odour of carbolic which, on occasions, fused with the patients' vomit. We'd do the rounds and the psychiatrist I was assigned to, wanting to get away for a gin and tonic in the pub next door, would give barely a lazy glance at his patients, yet say something as profound as, 'He probably felt he was being destroyed at birth, I dare say; too frightened to leave the womb and too scared to stay in it.' Then he'd turn his head to look at the nurses following us out of the ward and say, 'Good Lord, look at that one's tits, Norman.' The man was crawling on his bed. I tried to feel the pain.'

Robert could sense that he was, at least partly, feeling it as he spoke.

'Another patient, one who I was looking after, had pleaded for entrance at his local Bedlam where, on his first morning, he'd been led onto the wet grass in bare feet and asked by a male nurse if he bit his nails. 'We'll soon make you better,' he'd said. But he stayed months and put into insulin-deep sleeps because, as you know,' he frowned sarcastically, 'we don't drop 'em into cold baths any more. They'd play football, you may have heard of the game, carrying bottles of sugar water to drink to defy sudden comas and watch a crazed goalkeeper stopping shots with his face. They were told to dig the hospital allotments without knowing why, I didn't either, and someone from ward 4 would scrape a pick across a long-stay's scalp, blood covering his smiling teeth. And the stiff dances in the female ward with glazed eyed girls were no incentive for anyone to leave

CHAPTER TWO

their glass-walled minds, and their silent screams would be just as loud.'

He got up from his chair at the head of the long table, walked to the door behind him and turned back again. 'I'm telling you this because there may be one or two of you who go into psychotherapy and, perhaps, the idea of only clinical psychologists working in hospitals will, hopefully, be dropped and you can work in them; though I confess I don't know much about such places over here and I would think drugs are used more. But in case you do, you must take it seriously, must be... merciful.' He ended the seminar there and left the room.

Sitting there watching him and the others leave, Robert considered the idea of delving into a damaged or malformed psyche. It would mean watching someone over time struggling through, hopefully, to a psychic resurgence, a wellness; but knew also that for him it would largely be about his theorising and getting his and others insights confirmed. He considered for a moment his own make up and if he really would feel a sense of satisfaction, of achievement in helping somebody psychologically, helping mend them. There was a barren spot there, maybe because he didn't have a child; Jess had discovered early in their marriage that she couldn't conceive. He made his way out of the room, flippantly thinking that maybe he could use his experience of the world to specialise in the psychology of construction sites.

The day after finishing Finals he was walking across the campus to the coffee bar when he heard his name called. It was Norman Lee. Walking beside him he asked how he'd got on the previous day. After the early papers he'd told Robert, with mild but genuine concern, that, surprisingly, he wasn't doing that well and to let himself go, to forget the textbooks, use his own ideas. He had. He told Norman that he thought he'd pulled things around with the final paper and that the fact it was now all over hadn't quite emotionally kicked in yet.

'Understandable, I felt the same after mine. I wanted to talk to you about something. It's probably fanciful, but you were speaking recently of not having been to Britain and I wondered if you'd like the chance to. You've been a good student; I think you're aware of that.' He smiled a little mischievously. 'You also seem to be a fan of my views; apparently you've rather broadcast them around the faculty. Look, as you know, I'm returning home shortly, my contract was for two years only, anyway, and - '

'I'm glad I was here for them.'

'So am I, and I did think that maybe you could come with me. The new college I'm going to, which is, in effect, the provincial annexe of a London university, needs a temporary assistant lecturer in our subject.' Robert liked the 'our subject' part. 'I'll be staying with someone who I met as a student and who's been left an eighty acre farm; his father farmed it for years until he died recently, and has now taken it over. You may not want this nor feel ready for it, though with some work I think that you could be.' He grinned. 'I overheard two students in the same year as you the other day, one of them asking the other if he remembered you teaching them social psychology in their first term. I'm aware you were one of the few that came with prior knowledge of the subject, so, perhaps unconsciously, you were already practising pedagogy.'

He frowned. 'I don't even know whether or not you're married, do I.' Looking at his watch he said, 'I've got to be off now, but do think about it and we'll speak some more. I'm giving a talk on Piaget in the small hall tomorrow afternoon, you're not obliged to come of course, but maybe I'll see you in the student bar afterwards. I think they may even let me in,' he grinned, and hurried off towards the main exit of the campus.

Robert slowed his pace. He'd wrenched himself gladly out of his lifetime's milieu, from what he knew, had only known: the often cruel, but after long familiarity, strangely comforting workplace banter, people and places that had always been there, even his father, his mother having died years before, and Jess's family, how would she feel? But he'd now met and become part of an academic belonging, a kind of club, perhaps even an elite one, and now this, also, had gone, he'd said goodbye to Mick and Guy and Amber and a few of the others only yesterday. He hadn't really thought about what he wanted to do now that he had, he hoped, successfully graduated. It would be a failure to go back to what he'd always done. But, could he teach?

As he walked, his head filled with images of Regency houses in London, of cathedrals, stately homes in the shires and, too, of the Depression and the hunger marches that had taken place. He'd admired the workers there who had fought back four years before with similar marches and demonstrations for union recognition as

CHAPTER TWO

they had here. Rarely having been out of work himself or ever really actively opposing entrenched authority, except for a day's go-slow on a site, he felt a little guilty.

Another reminder of what seemed an increasingly distant past was he and Jess seeing Billy when recently walking through Murray Hill and asking him where he was working. He'd pointed behind him to a building with scaffolding around it.

'Just there, I'm doing first fixing at the mo. Hope to do some secondary when it's ready. I've been back to the Chrysler; bit o' maintenance and stuff. How's university?' He hadn't waited for an answer. 'Bit different, uh? Not like the palookas we've worked with. A lot of 'em are outta work again; it's not great. Gonna get a good degree? All the best, Rob, you too, Jess.'

He'd smiled and hurried off. Robert briefly watched him walk away and felt a twinge of sadness; a long episode, an era even, seemed to have gone.

He decided to tell Jess about Norman Lee's offer straight away. After some hesitation she seemed to take to the idea rapidly. Pragmatic as ever, she thought that if he did some teaching it would be a good start for him if he was going to become a lecturer or therapist or whatever he was going to do.

'Either way, it seems pretty good and I'd like to see England. Hey, you're supposed to have come from there, didn't your Grandpa Bob do some sort of research and found out that his family was from Cumberland or Northumberland or somewhere?'

Robert held her to him. 'Something like that.'

'When will it be?'

'We don't actually have to go when Lee does; we don't need to go with him. I dunno, say, in a month or so? That okay?'

'Sure.'

He was surprised at her quick acceptance; this wasn't her usual thinking it through, the weighing of pros and cons.

'Let's go to Maloney's and have some drinks.' she said.

'Let's look at the girder men photo.'

Somebody there mentioned Adolf Hitler. Robert was hearing the name increasingly and also remembered it from half a dozen years before when he'd read somewhere that the man had become German Chancellor and now, apparently, had invaded Prague. He thought little of it

CHAPTER 3

He knew the war had started because everybody was talking about it. It began when his father and mother sat bending their heads towards the wireless in the corner of the back room listening to what dad had called an 'important announcement.' He turned from the set after a while and noticing Keith earnestly sitting there had said, 'Well, it looks like we're at war, son.'

'Can I go out, now?' Keith asked his mum.

'Don't go far,' she said.

He went out and ran down the street to see if any of the Bowhays were in. It was exciting; there'd be tanks and guns and shells and soldiers and he wondered if there would still be school. After a while his mates began singing songs about it. They would be playing footie over the park or dribbling a tennis ball around the lamppost outside Wag's house when it would start. Terry might begin it with, 'Hitler has only got one ball, Himmler is sim'lar and Goebbels has no balls at all.' and then Kenny would sing, 'We'll hang out the washing on the Siegfried Line...'

One morning, when he didn't have to get up for school and mum had to leave for work early, aunt Flo invited him into her back room, gave him some breakfast and asked if he wanted to talk. He didn't know what to talk about. 'Suit yourself,' she said and got up from the table to wash the dishes singing quietly to herself, 'Because of Goring we've got to go whoring...' He didn't know what it meant.

There were always reminders of it. If he was helping his mother in the scullery with the washing, maybe putting the whites through the mangle, he would hear from the wireless words and places that were becoming familiar to him: Poland, U-boats, Molotov, Ribbentrop, and when he ran out of the house one afternoon shouting, 'Watch the demon bowler.' and had accidentally thrown his cricket ball through the fanlight of Mrs. Foxcroft's house opposite, she came out shouting, 'You cheeky little sod, I'll get the Germans onto you.'

Mum had made him go across to apologise to her. He did, beginning with, 'I'm sorry, Mrs. Fanlight lady.' before quickly correcting himself. He and his mates were always christening people with their own made up names: Mrs. Fish Shop lady, Mister Paper

CHAPTER THREE

Shop, Mister Butcher and, though he knew that a West Ham footballer owned the off licence, he was always Mister Off Licence.

The war never seemed to come. He heard things on the wireless, but it seemed mostly about governments and politics which he wasn't interested in. He, the Bowhays and sometimes Alfie and Mickey and a few others, would go to the park and, using branches as rifles or Tommy guns, split into pairs or groups, hide behind trees and bushes and shoot at each other. Sometimes, someone shouted out 'missed.' and ran to hide behind another tree. Mickey was always dong this when it was obvious he'd been shot. Keith always seemed to have to be a German, though didn't mind because he liked pretending dead, clutching at his heart and lying still. When they got tired of this it was back to tin can Tommy and odds and ends or, occasionally, going to Stratford and pinching penny 'Mighty Midget' books and aniseed balls from Woolworths.

He was copying a photo of a race horse and jockey from the sports page of the 'Mirror,' sketching a faint outline then other lines which he softened by rubbing a finger across them to give an 'illusion of depth,' Mrs. Glading his art teacher called it, when he heard it and knew that this time it was real. He'd listened to the practice sirens before, they'd been going on for some time, but he hadn't taken much notice. This time it somehow sounded louder and more demanding, though he wasn't sure what it wanted of him. Mum was next door at Mrs. Thornton's with Lenny, dad was at work and he didn't know what to do. He wanted someone there in the house; he would have liked uncle Harry to come down and talk to him, ask how his drawings were going or take him out to the air raid shelter he and dad had put up. His uncle had visited their back room nearly every evening for a week to talk to his dad about it before they got some spades and pickaxes and dug a big hole at the back of the garden. He watched them put it up and afterwards helped throw some earth on the top and sides, 'to camouflage it,' dad had said. A lorry full of curved, corrugated sheets of metal had come along the street dropping them off outside the houses.

He decided to go into the shelter. The siren was still wailing as he sat on one of the lower bunks where Lenny was supposed to sleep. Then he heard mum calling his name from inside the house. As he poked his head out, the back door opened and she came scurrying towards the shelter carrying his brother.

'Why didn't you come next door?' she shouted, 'I didn't know where you were.'

The three of them sat there quietly for a while then he heard some distant noises, he knew they were exploding bombs; they made a sound like 'crump,' but before the explosions there was sometimes a whistling noise; it was like Guy Fawkes Night with the screamer fireworks, but a lot louder and longer.

It went on for a long while and Lenny began crying. As it got dark his mother told him to hold Lenny and rock him.

'You know how to do it; I'll get us something to eat.'

She hurried out and into the scullery, but didn't switch on the light. He stood up and rocked Lenny in his arms until mum came back again with some soup, a cup of tea and a doorstop of bread and plum jam. He leaned out and could just see some flashes past the end of the street before mum shouted at him to get back in. He sat there before going to sleep drinking his soup and wondering why the crumps came after the flashes. The all-clear sound from the siren woke them as it got light. He couldn't wait to tell Alfie and the Bowhays about it and ask if they'd gone down the shelter, too.

Mum would knock on his door at night to wake him, carrying Lenny, though he did sometimes hear the siren and get up himself and follow them downstairs rubbing the sleep from his eyes. They went through the back room and scullery and into the garden. The shelter had an earthy smell and, though it was strange and the bunks were hard, there was a candle his mother lit which made it almost cosy and helped him to ignore the bangs and flashes outside. If his dad was home he'd be the last in to make sure they were all safely inside; sometimes he would lift Keith out of bed and carry him down. He knew he should have liked this because he was being protected, but didn't feel comfortable in his father's arms. If he was lying awake watching the flashing light from the bombs through the gaps around the metal door of the shelter, he'd put his head outside and perhaps hear a Junkers 88. He knew what aircraft it was because, just like Alfie and the others, he could recognise it by the sound of its engines. Sometimes he'd hear the ack-ack guns from the park where they'd put cinders down where the allotments had been and made a large shelter with a white 'S' on a black board at the front of it. There was a searchlight and a barrage balloon there, too; he thought it looked like a fat elephant without a trunk.

CHAPTER THREE

After nights of sitting in the shelter, Mickey from next door asked him if he wanted to come into their one. Keith asked his mum and she said it would be alright. As soon as the wailing began the next night she ushered him into the garden, lifted him over the wire mesh fence and lowered him into Mrs Barrett's. 'Thanks, Ruth, he'll be alright,' she said, pointing him to her shelter and then going back inside the house where she sat in a wire cage under the dining table. She didn't seem to have a husband; Keith wondered where Mickey's dad was and who'd built their shelter, he didn't remember it going up; maybe the council did it while he was at school. When he went in, Mickey was there with his sister who said he could use the same bunk as her. He'd never spoken to her before because she was so quiet and didn't seem to speak to anyone. It felt strange lying close to her and feeling her against him. He wanted to hold her, but could see his mother in his head frowning down at him and telling him it was wrong. He wondered if it was something else God could punish him for.

It seemed, after weeks of bombing, alright for him to sleep with aunt Flo, though, because mum said it was. She explained to him that as Harry was now on nights and Flo was on her own and felt nervous, it would comfort her. He never thought of asking why she or uncle Harry hardly ever came down the shelter. He started going upstairs at his bedtime and lay awake most evenings till she came to bed. He could feel her weight bump down next to him and would pull the sheets over his head and pretend to be asleep. He'd lie there hardly daring to move, hearing her breathing and her body still and quiet just inches from him in the blacked out room. He would lie on his back gazing at the ceiling, though it was too dark to be able to see it, and would gently turn towards her back. He wanted to touch it, just a little bit, touch her waist, her underwear, which mum called 'combs,' with his hand. Then she'd sigh and turn towards him, putting her hands under the pillow and sleep quietly and still again. He would turn away and try to sleep.

After a few nights of this he heard dad say to mum in the back room while he stood in the side entrance hanging his coat up, 'We've got to stop this, Ruth, I didn't want him to go up there in the first place. I told you, he's a bit too old for this sort of thing, she'll have to get used to being on her own at nights; she's an adult. I don't care how nervous she is, if she wants a bit of company in the evenings for an hour he can go up there before he goes to bed, but he's not staying with her all night.'

Aunt Flo told him in her scullery that evening that he wasn't to sleep with her anymore. That night, in his own bed, he dreamt that he was walking with her down Geere Road on his way to school when he realised he was dreaming. It was lovely, he could do what he wanted, anything, it didn't matter, it wasn't real. He poked his tongue out at some women with shopping bags walking on the other side of the street and as they frowned at him he shouted, 'Bollocks.' This was better than drinking Tizer straight from the bottle. He turned to aunt Flo and pulled her jacket off and undid her skirt, which was easy to do because he'd seen mum do hers, and then tried to undo her bra but couldn't. He didn't really know what he did then or what he was supposed to do, but it was exciting. He wanted to tell Alfie about it, but didn't see him next day and when he did, forgot to.

When it started again one afternoon soon afterwards the siren failed to go off. He was sitting in the armchair in the back room reading the comic strip in the 'Mirror' and wondering why Belinda kept saying, 'Great Jehosophat.' when the glass in the window moved across the room in front of him, seeming to almost float into the chimney breast. He knew it was a bomb; though the sound was so loud he didn't really hear it, just the noise of glass smashing and a vibrating sound in his head. He brushed bits of plaster and dust from the newspaper and looked through the gap where the window had been to the bath swinging like a giant pendulum on its nail in the fence. He went towards it and looked up at Mrs. Barrett's upstairs windows. They were the same as always. The front door opened and mum came in and asked if he was alright. Her face looked strange.

'Where's the window?' she asked.

While he was still watching the bath slowly rocking to a stop, mum rushed upstairs to get his brother, but the all-clear started so she came down again and they cleared up most of the room between them. He asked if he could go out to see what had happened. His mother went outside with him and they heard Anthony Cohen's mum, who was always chasing him and his mates away from the lamp post outside her house, screaming for her son, who everybody called Wag. She kept calling his name. Mum walked up to her, slapped her face and she stopped screaming. Then Anthony walked down from the top of the road towards them; he'd been in a friend's

CHAPTER THREE

house. Keith looked down the street to where the Bowhays were standing outside their house.

'Go down to the Bowhays then, but don't go any further, and be careful,' his mother said.

He ran down to them to see what they were looking at. From the end of the street to the main road where the small cinema and the corner pub was, and where he would watch the eels being cut up on a slab outside, the pieces still moving about, was a field of smoke and dust. He couldn't see any buildings through it and there was no sound. There were people on the other side of the road looking at it, also, just standing there. Doris Hill was there and Iris and skinny Gwen with their mother. Nobody was saying anything and Gwen started playing hopscotch. He then heard the bells of fire engines and ambulances from the Portway and two fire engines came down the turning towards the smoke. He'd never seen a fire engine in his street before and only seen two cars; one belonging to Doctor Murphy, the other to Wendy's father which was outside his house all week till Sunday when he'd drive Wendy and her mum to the seaside.

When the fog of smoke and dust started to clear he could just make out some buildings and houses through it, though not as many as there had been. He couldn't quite see the cinema and the row of shops next to it nor the pub and the public baths. Kenny then started walking across the road towards the dust. Keith hurried behind him. As they turned by the Jew shop with its smashed window, Alfie Herd came towards them through the rubble carrying something. He saw them and grinned, lifting it high above his head. It was a wooden leg. In the other hand he was holding a bra, one of the cups filled with mud and bits of brick. He gave his strange grin again - mum once said he looked like a Mongol - and started swinging it around his head. Keith thought of his Sunday school lessons and a picture of David fighting Goliath. He showed them a bag of shrapnel he'd collected which he carried about with him for weeks afterwards.

As he was going to bed that evening his father came in the front door looking worried.

'You all okay then, son? I heard it was down Plaistow way, heard we caught a packet.'

He rested his hand on Keith's head for a second then went through to his wife, closing the back room door. He began talking to her, asking if Lenny was alright. Keith, looking through the frosted glass door panels, heard them talking, but they weren't standing near each other.

Next day he went by himself to see the debris, though telling his mother he wouldn't go there but play over the park. There were police, air raid wardens, fire engines and people walking about looking down at the ground and occasionally bending to pick something up. He guessed that they used to live there and wondered if he'd see someone hopping along looking for a wooden leg. He looked along Leebon Street; a half of one side of it wasn't there anymore, except for a whole inside of a house with wallpaper and pipes and a fireplace showing; there was also a toilet bowl hanging down. As he walked further towards the main road wondering what had happened to the eels, he saw a man in a dress wearing high heels and doing a sort of dance on the bricks and mud. He had a curly wig and was wearing lipstick. Some older boys were there and began shouting at him, jeering and calling him names, none of which Keith understood. As they surrounded him the wig slid down his face and onto the ground and they jeered even louder. Keith felt his fists clench and ran forward shouting, 'Stop it.' As the boys turned to him he saw that one of them was Frankie Nutt and also recognised a boy from Geere Road. As the man ran away, some of the boys threw bits of brick and wood at Keith. They then moved on into the main road towards the school which was still standing there high above the houses.

He made his way back and passed a house with its front door caved in and a piece of paper stuck on the porch saying, 'Don't bother to knock.' There was blood trickling down his forehead and he felt small and skinny and lost. It reminded him of the week before when he'd been passing the off licence and saw two girls hitting a little boy and he'd also told them to stop. He couldn't understand why they were doing it. One of hem had picked up a piece of glass from a smashed beer bottle and thrown it at his face, hitting him at the side of his eye, but it hadn't bled. When he got home now and his mother saw the blood on his forehead he told her he'd been climbing a tree and had fallen out of it.

A week later, he, mum and Lenny stayed at his mother's friend's house in Barnet for a weekend to 'get away from it all,' his dad said. Lenny also slept through the explosion of a parachute mine that dropped on the corner house of the street they were in; he seemed to sleep through anything, like Bluey. They came home right away.

CHAPTER THREE

He was in the back garden a few days afterwards when he heard distant engines and the sound of a plane diving. He looked up and watched two Spitfires high in the sky chasing a Messerschmitt until they disappeared behind the park. He knew what plane they were after because he'd seen a picture of it on a cigarette card. He'd also seen diagrams of manoeuvres used in air battles in his 'Blackout Book' which had black pages and fluorescent words and pictures so he didn't need to have the light on in his bedroom to read it because, as dad said, chinks of light might be showing and could be seen by the night bombers. The Air Raid warden would probably bang on the front door as well. He sometimes wondered if the Germans had the same book because they would then know how to fight the Spitfires.

The next day he was chalking Bluey's name on his shell when he heard a roaring, clacking sound from the end of the street that got louder very quickly and saw a Messerschmitt fighter flying low over the back gardens towards him. He stood there staring at it until aunt Flo came running into the garden and threw herself on top of him as bullets went into the grass and bits of wood from the fences and glass from windows fell around them. Then it was quiet again. She lay on him for a while before she got up, asked if he was alright then went back indoors.

If there was no school, he played over the debris most days though his mum preferred him to be inside with her so that she knew where he was. Lenny had begun crawling, but mostly backwards, which made him laugh, so he liked him a bit more now. Mum and dad didn't laugh much except when 'Workers Playtime' was on the wireless, especially when a lady said, 'It's being so cheerful that keeps me going.' and someone kept asking, 'Can I do you now, sir?' and when they went to uncle Reg's and he told them jokes. He remembered one of them and told it to Alfie.

'There's an air raid on and this man in the shelter has to come out of it to go to the lavatory. So he does, and while he's in there the house takes a direct hit. He staggers out and goes into the road where an ARP man asks him if he's okay. He says, 'I only pulled the chain and the bleedin' 'ouse fell down.'

Grown ups liked saying, 'bleedin',' he'd noticed.' Alfie did, too. He came running out of his house one day shouting, 'Sister Anna will carry the banner. But she's in the family way. She's in everybody's bleedin' way.' and ran off down the street still carrying his bag of shrapnel.

Mum never seemed to laugh much and never did when cousin Vera came round and fed her baby. She'd sit in the chair opposite him while he looked at her breast till mum told him not to. 'Look somewhere else,' she'd snap. When he was playing over the debris there were two houses that were still intact and sometimes, at the back of them, he saw two men talking to each other over the garden fence which was twisted flat and reminded him of the roller coaster at the Kursaal. They both smoked pipes and one would say something to the other who would nod a lot and then they'd do it in reverse. They didn't seem to be surprised that the houses around them weren't there anymore, they didn't appear to notice; they just held their pipes and nodded.

At school they didn't talk about the bombs much, just went to their lessons: maths, which he didn't like and English and art which he did; he still got red stars put on his drawings, especially when he started sketching spitfires with their machine guns firing bullets through propeller circles at Stuka dive bombers.

He was still small, but knew he would get bigger when he was older and tried to take no notice of boys telling him he ought to put horse dung in his shoes to make him look taller or eat more stews, though got fed up with younger boys looking down at him sometimes and calling him 'Little Keefie Clements.' Cousin Roy called him 'Titch.' Dad would take him to Wickford, in Essex, sometimes to see a lady he called Aunt Em who was a large, fat woman with sons who had big red faces and were always laughing. He often thought they were laughing at him. One of them was called Boy; his real name was William, but that was what his father called him so everyone did.

A lad in his year at school, but in a different class, who lived in Leebon Street where, his mum said, the rough boys came from, laughed at him once and every time the bell rang to let them know it was time to change classrooms, Keith would run out of his class to find him. He would punch him and pull his hair and would be punched back. They did it after all their lessons that day. If he found him coming out of the chemistry lab he would wrestle with him, noticing a smell like bad eggs as he did so; he could still smell it when the bell went for home time.

Sometimes he forgot that the war wasn't just about being bombed, but about soldiers and airmen as well, like when he was with his mum in Romford Market and a lorry with a tarpaulin over the back

CHAPTER THREE

of it stopped suddenly at the kerb in front of them and one of the men in blue uniforms standing under it fell forward on his face onto the road. He looked up as the men jumped down to help him and Keith could see the veins in his face like a map of red rivers and streams. It frightened him.

When he woke next morning there was a nasty smell in his bed and the top of his leg felt slimy and slippery. He knew what he'd done, but didn't know what to do. When his mother knocked on the door to wake him he kept where he was, very still. She knocked again after a while.

'You gettin' up, Keith, or gonna stay there all day? You'll grow roots if you lay there much longer.'

A few minutes afterwards she opened the door. 'What's the matter? You getting up or what? Don't you feel well?' He turned his face into the pillow. 'What's happened then, anybody been picking on you at school?'

She stood over him for a while then went out of the room. She came back again shortly afterwards.

'You getting up then or what?'

He shook his head and she went out. He lay there, not moving, pretending that nothing had happened, it wasn't real. After some time, there was a knock on his door and he heard a quiet, 'Hello, Keith.' It was Joan from next door. He liked her better than her sister Peggy, she had fair hair and used to tickle him under his chin and say, 'Who's a pretty boy, then?' She'd started it a long while ago, but hadn't done it much lately. He felt his bed bounce as she sat on the foot of it.

'What have you done?' she asked gently. 'Have you done a number two?' He shook his head again, still pushed into the pillow. 'It's not worse is it?' She chuckled. He felt her hands on the back of his shoulders. 'Come on, turn over and stand up and we'll wash you.' He could feel her breath on his neck.

'It's alright, I won't tell anyone,' she whispered.

She went out and returned with a bowl of warm water and a flannel, he could feel the steam; it smelt nice. He held his sheet around him and stood up with his eyes shut. The sheet was gently taken away and he felt warm water around his hips and bum. She dried him with a towel.

'You can open your eyes now. We'll just get this bedding off and your mother can wash it. I can see why you didn't want her to see it.

It's okay though, these things happen. Better get dressed then come in the back room.'

When he did she'd already gone. He knew it was nice of her to do what she had, but he didn't want to speak to her again. His mother said nothing, just spat on her hand and slicked his hair down. 'You look like the wreck of the Hesperus,' she said. In the afternoon he walked to the far end of the park and laid face down on the grass, wanting to push himself through the earth. Sometimes he'd do this when his mum and dad argued, but at those times he'd go further away to the recreation ground.

His father took him to a friendly match between Chelmsford and West Ham one Saturday; there were no more games at the Boleyn because of the war. Dad wore the cap he did when he went to the pub. It made his face look small, like his own; 'Farthing face.' he'd heard aunt Elsie call him. They caught a bus to Stratford Station then a train. When they got off there seemed as many people as at the speedway and they were carried along with them. They nearly all wore caps, like a uniform. He wondered why Wendy's dad didn't wear one, he wore a trilby. Mum said he was, 'in business.' He called for Wendy once and as she opened the door he saw her dad kissing her mum in the back room. It scared him. He'd never seen his dad do that to his mum, ever.

During the game his father explained what was happening, but he understood a lot of it and saw players doing things with the ball that he hadn't done before and wanted to practice over the park with the others when they played five-a-side if there were enough of them. He had a claret and blue scarf that he wore for speedway, but didn't wave it here like he did when watching the bikes.

At half time he had some crisps, while his dad had a pie with lots of tomato sauce on which made Keith feel sick just watching him eat it. He'd use vinegar, too, to put on the cockles and whelks he and uncle Albert had outside 'The Crown.' in Elm Park, ripping them with his teeth and spitting bits out. Keith hated the smell of vinegar; sometimes he felt giddy just smelling it in the fish shop. He'd wait till the shop was nearly empty before getting cod and chips and his mother would moan at him again for taking so long to get their meal. He always had to sit at the table in the back room and wait till everyone had finished before leaving it and then, perhaps, go over the park and play in the sandpit which mum had told him not to because he could get nits from it.

CHAPTER THREE

For a while he saw a lot of Alfie and they began playing a game where they would go to the phone box in the main road, look in the directory to find the numbers of shops that did domestic repairs such as mending vacuum cleaners or electrical goods and ask them to come to an address in their street of someone neither of them liked. Alfie paid for the calls and did the talking while Keith searched through the directory. Remembering what happened on the debris, Keith asked Alfie to arrange for someone to come to Frankie Nutt's house to fix his mother's typewriter. Sitting on a garden wall opposite her house they almost fell off it laughing when a van stopped and Frankie's mum, looking bewildered, then angry, argued with the driver. The boys doubted whether she even had a typewriter. They also began playing 'knock down ginger,' where they would knock on a front door and scoot away down the street and hide in a front garden. Tiring of this, they got some twine and one of them, usually Keith, would quietly tie a length of it to a door knocker, run it across the road and connect the other end to the knocker of the house opposite. When they got the hang of this and knocked and ran, the person who lived there would open the door causing the opposite knocker to lift and, as the door was closed, that knocker would fall, and so on. The best bit was seeing people's faces as they went to their gates and looked up and down the road seeing no-one, except two boys pointlessly kicking their heels into a wall they were sitting on some houses away. They stopped this activity soon afterwards when a motor bike drove through the thread.
   He couldn't quite describe it, but things seemed to have changed, though they still had bubble and squeak every Monday and his dad still looked like a rabbit eating cabbage at mealtimes. He didn't understand why his father sat him on his lap one evening, facing him forward, putting his hands under his armpits, asking if he was comfortable then suddenly opening his legs and catching him just before he hit the floor. His father ruffled his hair and said, 'Let that be a lesson, son; don't trust anyone.' And he never saw the man with the horse and cart with a small roundabout on it which uncle Charlie called a carousel that you could ride on for a penny or two empty jam jars. His mother seemed to laugh even less these days, too, and they hadn't been to aunt Con's for a long while either and there was no Escalado any more. It was a good job he had aunt Gwen.
   He finished another drawing of a spitfire with tracer bullets and the pilot's face seen through the circles he drew with his HB pencil

and sat there watching a fly stuck to the sticky brown paper tape hanging from a roll pinned to the ceiling. He could see its stuck wings and moving legs as if it was crawling upside down in the air. For a second he was the fly. He didn't like the war anymore.

 She was in the shelter with Keith and Lenny; it had been quiet since the siren half an hour ago and they were both asleep. Two hours previously she had used an eyebrow pencil to paint a thin line from high up the back of Flo's legs down to her heels, after her sister-in-law had rubbed gravy browning on them, to make it look as if she was wearing stockings. She had seen a pair of nylons herself recently, but they were on the black market and she couldn't afford them. Nothing, it seemed, could stop Flo and her fashions, she liked wearing blouses fitted at the waist with a belt, high heeled shoes and she seemed to wear a lot of red, sometimes the same shade as her lipstick. She thought about Gwen and wondered if she was in her shelter. Albert probably wasn't, he was like that; he'd say smugly that if Jerry's bombs didn't have his number on 'em he'd be alright, and occasionally take a stroll to the pub even if the siren had gone. Because he was in France in the last war, he'd sometimes say to Gwen, 'Parlay voo mamzell, lah prominard.' She liked him saying that and would always smile at him when he did.

 She looked in the direction of where Fred worked south of the Thames and wondered what he felt coming home from work and seeing the sky red from the fires, though she wasn't sure whether, from Kidbrooke, he could see as far away as where they lived. No wonder he seemed so browned off these days. He worked in Security on an estate of government warehouses where he patrolled around having to be in a certain building at a particular time to see if everything was as it was when he last looked. But, there was overtime occasionally and they could do with the money, Lord knows, what with the cost of food and Keith's clothes, though he did get free milk and cheap dinners at school, and there was Fred's fares to work and having to rely on other people to look after Lenny, though Gwen did it willingly enough and so did Peggy when she could, but she felt she had to treat them sometimes.

 Although it was a relief that the raids hadn't been so heavy for a couple of nights, she knew it could change at any time. If there was a raid or threat of one during the day and Keith was at school he'd be sent down to its basement with the other children and, if she was at

CHAPTER THREE

work, which was quite near the school, she would go into the shelter next to the factory with the other workers and as soon as the all-clear went hurry home to Peggy or get a train to Gwen's, whoever was looking after Lenny. She felt tense all the time; waiting, worrying, expecting that horrible whining from the sirens again and the sound of explosions, and it didn't help that Fred was on nights again; though he was probably safer there than she was. They weren't too far from the docks and she knew the Luftwaffe was gunning for them. A friend of hers in Canning Town lived in a street running down to the docks with large boats at the end of it. It was strange to stand in her back garden and look up at the funnels and the huge black sides of a ship.

The small factory where she worked now made toys, but the government had stopped the supply of metal to it so now they were making mostly wooden ones or soft toys like dolls and teddy bears. It meant a bit of variety for her, though she sometimes wished she was making munitions like Elsie was. She felt a little guilty that she wasn't helping the war effort and she also liked the turban and tight white smock her sister-in-law wore there; she thought she might look quite good in them.

She looked down at Keith, though he was just a shape, there was no light, the torch batteries had run out and she'd forgotten to get more candles. She knew that the situation couldn't be doing him much good; he never seemed to want to be indoors, always wanting to be outside, though perhaps he would have been like it anyway. There were places to play other than the debris and he did go over the park, but not as much as he used to. He never seemed to draw the things he once did, either, like trees and racing cars and mountains; now it was all tanks and airplanes firing guns and something he did the other day that looked like a bombed-out house with bits of picture rails and fireplaces hanging from it, and there was a little girl standing on the ground looking up and pointing at it. She remembered when she had to take him to Queen Mary's Hospital to have his adenoids and tonsils out when he was younger and the doctor had said, 'My God, look at that child's eyes, mother, they're so bright.'

She supposed he was intelligent enough, with his books and the way he drew things, but he didn't say much to her or Fred; not like Reg's boy, he was always talking to him and Glad and he seemed to laugh a lot, too. But Keith had his friends, though Alfie was a strange one, but with a mother like that she wasn't surprised; fortunately, he didn't seem friendly with any of the Leebon Street lot. He did sometimes come home late and rarely say where he'd been and she was sure he hadn't been with his friends, either; though she was loathe to punish him because of the war.

She'd recently begun wondering if it was good for him to be growing up where they were, not that she or Fred could do anything about it. She would like to live where Gwen and Doll were down the line, the people there weren't rough and were better mannered, nicer, not like Teapot Lil from 56 with her coming round and cadging tea or a bit of sugar, and she was such a gossip. They can cause trouble, people like that, with their slander; she ought to be reported. She did have a sneaking suspicion, though, that some of them might look down on her, but then, a lot of them were probably all fur coats and no drawers; but she was sure they didn't swear so much, except Albert. He called the people in the caravans in the fields at the back of Doll's, 'gyppos' and had a silly joke he kept repeating, 'She was only petrol pump assistant, but she knew the smell of Benzole.' She'd also heard him refer to someone as a 'cowson,' a word she hated. Gwen had moaned to her about him the other day, saying that he was talking of the young man next door to them who was seeing an older woman, and had said, 'If he gets anywhere near 'er she'll suck him in and blow him out in bubbles.' She couldn't understand why her sister had married him. And some of the expressions Keith's friends used, like, 'shut yer cake 'ole.' and 'nob head.' she thought ugly. She'd heard Keith the other day on the door step say to Alfie, 'Why is Green Street like a pig's arse? 'cos it's got West Ham on one side and East Ham on the other.' She told him off for it. The air was fresher where her sisters lived anyway, and most of the houses had trees as well as hedges in their front gardens which were larger than theirs with its little bit of privet and a few flowers she'd grown. But, as she often said, it's not where you live, it's how you live.

The Government was still talking about evacuation and, aware that they lived in an 'evacuable area,' she thought that she and Fred should think about it seriously, though it was hard to accept that her first born child would be safer away from her, but there'd been hardly a let up recently, it seemed incessant. Most of the parents didn't want their children to go and she didn't want Keith to, either, but they'd had to sit in the shelter night after night listening to the explosions and she knew how worried Fred was. She peeked out

CHAPTER THREE

sometimes at the red sky over the City; rumours had gone around that St. Paul's had been hit, but it hadn't. She thought Keith looked so miserable at times, and Fred wasn't helping matters, either. He seemed to be getting more and more irritated with him and he didn't appreciate the way Gwen looked out for him.

'She thinks the sun shines out of his bleedin' arse,' he'd said to her the other day when Keith had shown them the packet of sweets her sister had given him from the Jew shop.

The two of them were in the back room recently and when she went in Keith was sitting in the armchair drawing something on his drawing board and Fred was talking to him, but he wouldn't look up from what he was doing, just nodded his head. She could see Fred getting angry so suggested to Keith that he go out and that she'd seen Alfie outside. As he went out and the front door banged shut, Fred had smashed his fist down on the biscuit tin with the country cottage she liked painted on its lid and shouted, 'That bleedin' boy.' and, ignoring her, went out to the lavatory and sat there smoking a roll-up. When he came back in she would ask him to make enquiries at the local Education Authority or the Council offices, or she could ask Doll, she'd know what to do. She would miss her son, but she'd still have Lenny.

CHAPTER 4

They docked at Southampton aboard the SS Marie Duval three weeks after an uneventful, four day Atlantic crossing from New York and three weeks after Norman Lee had made the same journey. They took a train to Paddington where they stayed overnight before travelling to Norfolk. Though rarely journeying outside of New York City they were more familiar with the high ceilings and tables and chairs of the city railways than to a dingy brown carriage compartment that had two rows of grubby, upholstered benches and a small window that opened by pulling a leather strap. They sat opposite each other by the window; the middle aged woman in the far corner with a hat, brogue shoes and newspaper and not acknowledging them, caused Robert to think he may have mistakenly wandered onto a British film set. The small fields they looked out on had the occasional copse of trees, horse-drawn ploughs and ubiquitous hedges. It was pretty, but too neat and bounded; it felt contained. He had difficulty imagining what would constitute wilderness in such a place. As they passed farmhouses he also wondered what the one they were going to live in would be like.

They'd arranged to spend a day in London before meeting with Norman Lee; Jess had met him just the once, when they'd all had a meal together soon after they'd decided to join him abroad. She'd been unusually animated during it, excited at the prospect of living in another country. The owner of the farmhouse, he'd told them, was in France where he owned a *gitte* that he occasionally let to English holidaymakers, leaving the farming concerns at home to a foreman who had been there for years. Jess was optimistic about getting a job using her office skills, perhaps in Norwich, which wasn't far away from where they would be staying, or even at the university.

London was dirty and crowded and the buildings needed cleaning. The buses and trams looked strange and all the men seemed to wear hats: flat, peaked caps, bowlers, those that looked like small fedoras, and the women, unless they were wearing headscarves, wore small or wide brimmed ones; the girls were hatless and the boys in gabardine shorts, not jeans. There were lots of horse-drawn carts and far fewer cars than at home, Robert noticing that none of their drivers wore caps. This was the country that had influenced Marx so much, a

CHAPTER FOUR

country, as Norman would say, of recognisable symbols of pernicious class inequality, recognised here rather more fully than the psychic denial of much of America's populace.

Jess said she liked it, she felt at home, people were friendly; it had a familiar Bronx shabbiness, especially east of Aldgate Pump where they wandered through long, huddled, brick terraces where each side of a street looked like one long house with lots of doors. There was brick everywhere; he had never seen so much of it. In a pub, quickly adapting to the bland taste of jellied eels, but not to the warm beer, he mentioned it to a local who happened to be a builder and who told him they were called London bricks, Robert's interest interrupted by Jess telling him she was hungry again. They went to a nearby cafe and were intrigued by the culinary vernacular of 'airship on a cloud' for sausage and mash and 'babies on a raft' for beans on toast.

They were there, as Jess put it, to get the feel of the 'real' city. Robert, trying not to cross-examine her on why the poor should be more real than the rich or whether making vests in a sweatshop had more ontological validity than clipping the tip off a cigar, suggested they go to a local music hall. The walk there seemed a stereotype of Hollywood London Town: the buses, trams, the soot-ingrained buildings, raggedy assed kids, even the fog had made an appearance, deepening the dusk. Inside the theatre he had difficulty understanding the accents of both audience and performers, he more than Jess. In their hotel room later he thought through the day and was vaguely aware, in recalling the potpourri of sounds and scents, that there was the beginning of a minor fascination for the place.

The next morning they caught a train to Norwich where Norman Lee was waiting for them at the end of the station platform.

'It's good to see you Robert, both of you. How are you, Jess? Rather different from when we met at that bar of yours and I tried to persuade your husband to come.'

'Maloney's; and it didn't take much persuading.'

'Good. I suppose you've heard that war's finally been declared; it was announced a short while ago, inevitable, really. Nice way to be introduced to the place, I must say, but there it is.' He looked at Robert. 'I don't know what your government's reaction will be, but...'

'I don't think they'll want any part of it.'

'It'll just confirm to them, I suppose, that Europe consists merely of warring feudal states. We'll just have to see.' He looked at both of them. 'No one would blame you for a moment if you took the next train back to London and went home. It would be a great pity, but...' He looked at them questioningly. Jess firmly shook her head.

'There's your answer,' said Robert.

'Fine. Come, give me one of your cases.'

They travelled to Dereham on a train even older than the one they'd just left and from there Norman drove them in a small car to the farmhouse. He got out and opened the low wooden gate at the entrance of a long, part cinder, part grass drive which led into the yard at the side of a Georgian farm building, the castellated extensions on either side of it, Robert guessed, being Victorian. As they drew nearer, it was the proportions of the classic twelve-paned windows and their relationship to the pale grey stucco'd mass that pleased him. He wanted to point these things out to Jess and the feelings he got from them and idly wondered, as he had before, whether he'd seen pictures as a child of various houses and buildings and was searching for what they represented, though not sure what it was. He guessed there would be a rather glazed eyed response from her.

As they halted they saw a milking parlour in front of them and at the far side of the house, an orchard. They walked across cobbles to a door leading to a kitchen, off which was, as their host termed it, the long room. He turned to them.

'It's nice to have people here, especially you two.'

They told him they were glad to be here. Robert noticed the period furniture in the kitchen and an incongruous art deco lampshade in the long room as they were led through it into a room with a shuttered window then through to the staircase, its curving steps and handrail and tall ecclesiastical window, which he'd already spotted from the courtyard, was grandness on a minor scale. A bedroom at the top of it with en suite bathroom was for him and Jess, the room in a ground floor extension was Norman's.

He started work at the college three weeks afterwards, a time in which he and his wife spent walking around the farm, occasionally waving to the foreman sitting on his tractor, visiting the village's local thatched roof pub with beer that was just as warm as London's, visiting a crumbling Jacobean monastery and generally settling in, Jess even learning, after a fashion, to milk a cow, denying, despite her husband's wry smile, that it held any unconscious sexual content. She had started looking for a job the day after they'd arrived and had, similar to her previous experience, managed to get one in the admin department of the institution he would be working for.

None of his students had done the subject before and Robert was nervous, but also full of an almost zealous drive to inform them, to create an eagerness for his subject, though aware that they would be distracted, as was everyone, by what was going on around them; in the village, the college, in the press, on the radio, was a tenseness, a quiet, but troubled anticipation of what could happen to the country.

He was to teach the sociology component of the subject, the psychology more the province of Norman Lee. The main building was only two years old, its unfinished ancillary giving him a not uncomfortable feeling of déjà vu as he saw its crane from the bus on his first day there. It was a rather timid attempt at the moderne with a few areas of painted render, but mostly brick, its windows more neo-Georgian than curved sun trap. The students were, as he'd guessed, mainly provincial middle class, though there was a smattering of those with rural backgrounds and also a few older ones. He'd never heard a Norfolk accent before, the favourite word seeming to him to be 'boo'ful,' but was sure that his own, despite the popularity here of films such as 'Boys Town' and 'Angels with Dirty Faces' wasn't always readily understood either, though he did make an effort to practice sounding his consonants and to tone down his 'R's.' There was only one large lecture theatre, most lectures and all of the seminars taking place in classrooms.

He was surprised in his introductory lesson to see a black female student. There hadn't been that many black families in his home neighbourhood and there weren't many more people of that ethnicity on construction sites; though a black tradesman from Missouri he'd worked with for a few months was the best carpenter he'd known, better than himself, and there were fewer still at Reisler. The girl was clearly African.

He would liked to have made the impact that Norman Lee had in his first lecture in New York, but decided to be less controversial and began, other than telling them that he hoped they'd get used to his accent pretty quickly, by asking them to try to accept the idea that humans are largely a creation of their internalization of values, and that behaviour we almost automatically regard as 'natural' isn't; it's learnt. He asked them what they thought sociology was and received expected replies offering examples of what the subject did, not what it was, and explained that, essentially, the discipline was just another way of looking at the world. As a rider he told them to question everything.

The African girl put her hand up. 'Does that include what *you* say, also?'

'Yes, especially me, and there's no need to put your hand up, you're not at school.'

She smiled bashfully.

'Would you say that was a natural thing to do?'

She thought for a while. 'No.' she said it so quietly he hardly heard her. 'It's learned.'

'Quite. Let's look at some theories.'

Over the next few weeks, outlining paradigms such as functionalism, he moved on to Marx as a weapon against the shallow, accepting conservatism of the former's analogy of social institutions as bodily organs working for the good of the whole.

'When looking at institutions you must ask in whose interest they exist; for all equally or the few?'

Following a slight pause, half of them almost in unison said, 'The few,' while another, asking for the definition of 'good,' said, 'Isn't it rather arbitrary?'

'I knew from the start this class was bright when I said 'Good morning.' and no-one wrote it down.'

After giving them a Marxian based definition of the social hierarchy he asked them for the signs and symbols of the lower tiers. An ex-accountant had suggested it was the walk; a Doctor's son that it was the 'Daily Sketch' sticking out the back pocket of a boiler suit while another mentioned them using the public bar and not the saloon. Robert then, recalling a drinker he'd seen in a London pub, turned his back on them, bounced on his heels, squared his shoulders and asked the blackboard for, 'Two stouts, mate,' doubting whether he'd accurately captured the accent. He then asked if they thought he was mimicking the son of an Emeritus Professor of Literature at Oxford or a labourer, apologising for the stereotypes. It got a cheap laugh, but made the point. They continued offering visible clues of the manual, non-manual divide using ownership or not of cars as an obvious one, along with leisure activities and musical tastes, with the African girl breaking a nearly two week silence by suggesting that speech and appearance were the obvious signals.

He finished it there and, after telling them he'd see them the following week, wiped the board and gathered his notes while they

CHAPTER FOUR

left. As he was about to do so, he saw the African girl standing rather shyly against the far wall. She seemed somehow taller and slimmer than he had noticed, her rather frizzy, almost boyish hair accentuating it, looking more exotic, perhaps, than when with the others. He asked her if she wanted something. She moved towards him as he stood by his desk.

'To help me, if you would, choose an essay title. I think the answer to, 'Is social class inevitable in a capitalist society?' a bit obvious in that the particular political and economic system involved *means* a systematic inequality and an unequal distribution of resources. But maybe the quote you gave, 'If an individual defines his situation as real it's real in its consequences.' would be more interesting.'

'Up to you.'

'Meaning, I suppose, that subjective impressions are acted upon, influence behaviour.' Her voice, though still quiet, seemed firmer than he'd heard it before.

'Quite, but where do these subjective impressions come from? Are not most of them given to us by the social world?'

'Is that all we are then, the clichéd, 'product of our environment?' And what of what you called the 'massive confrontation of face-to-face reality.' That's the pinnacle of subjective impact isn't it?'

He'd awarded her a decent mark for her first essay, but this was her being more confident and critical. He wasn't sure whether to continue with this or head for home. He wanted to continue.

'I need to go, but I think you've just talked yourself into answering your original query.'

She smiled. 'Alright.'

He held the door for her. 'See you next week then, Prudence.'

'That's the first time you've used my Christian name.' The accent was very light.

'It's a Victorian name, isn't it?'

'Yes, along with the other virtues; mercy, hope, patience, etcetera, but then, if you evangelise a whole continent you have social and economic control, don't you.'

There was a slight, sardonic, almost matronising twinkle in her eyes.

'Yep, you sure do. I guess the Brits tried it on my country, too, and when I look at the Republican's 'Family, flag and prayer' I'm inclined to say they succeeded. Okay, I'm, going. Ciao.'

Leaving the building and walking across the lawn he couldn't quite understand why he hadn't, at least, accompanied her out. He wondered if her classmates talked to her much; he'd seen them mostly leave the room either silently or, after a particularly interesting seminar, talking loudly amongst themselves and her usually walking behind. He hadn't asked about her background. He would next time.

At the weekend he and Jess took a train to Hunstanton, wandered around some Gothic revival buildings and, at Jess's insistence, took a chilly walk across the beach and watched the sunset from one of the few towns in the county where it could be seen across the sea. They were gradually getting used to the flatness of the place, and also Wall's ice cream.

On Monday, after a quick chat in Norman's office to arrange his lecture subjects for the next few weeks, he went to the refectory. He collected his food from the counter and sat on his own just inside the door.

'Why don't you want to sit with me, because I'm a student? A female? Coloured? I've seen you sit with the others occasionally.'

She was standing just behind him. She smiled teasingly down and sat herself opposite.

'Isn't that kind of insulting, implying that I judge a person merely by their skin colour?'

She spoke quickly. 'Not at all, just that you're aware that the relevant norms in this context suggest that it's not good for a white person to sit next to or be seen with a black person and that it's considered to be worse for a white female with a black male. It's almost unconscious isn't it, but it was, unthinkingly, perhaps your first response. I'm not saying that -'

He held his hands up. 'Okay. Two things to say here: one, it's seen, certainly in the States, as more untenable for a white female because the black male could be perceived by others as threatening and seeing the woman as, probably, a sexual object; for the white male the perceptions are that a black woman *is* an object of sex. Secondly, it's yet another confirmation of the strength of early conditioning, the rest, arguably, merely veneers. And, to add a third, I didn't see you. Is that okay?'

'Yes. I'm trying to get under your skin, I suppose.

'Whatever its colour?'

'Are you going to get me a tea?'

CHAPTER FOUR

He did and, sitting again, asked her why she was trying to be provocative.

'I've little social life. I think that's why.'

He asked her if she saw any of the other students outside of college. She shook her head. He enquired about her background. She told him she was the daughter of an attaché to the Ambassador of her country, Kwa Zulu Province, at their Embassy in London; it was the first time the country had sent an Ambassador here. Her father had suggested she get a degree; he wanted her to do Law as he had; she, one of the social sciences. She'd spent her early educational years in Durban and was now living in a boarding house in Ripton.

'Why come here, why not go to a university in London?'

She grinned. 'I think my father was worried that I would get into mischief if I stayed there. Anyway, I've interrupted your lunch and I do have your essay to get on with.'

'It's okay, I'm not -'

'The library calls, bye bye.'

She walked quickly away and out the door. He looked at the back of it. She'd left a scent; it was fragrant, but strong. It seemed to settle deep in his nostrils.

After a weekend in which he and Jess went to Oulton Broads, refusing Norman's offer to take them in his car and travelling by coach, he jokingly accusing them of 'turning native,' Robert chose Deviance as his next topic. After explaining the difference between legal and illegal deviancy, he asked them - knowing he should keep it till after the theories just to confirm that as we were all deviants or potential ones what was the point of theorizing anyway - if any of them had ever committed a deviant act. At least half the class, Prudence's minimal shake of the head included, said no. He asked those in that percentage if they'd ever not paid their train or bus fares or taken sweets without paying when they were kids. Most smiled to themselves. He then asked them all to tell him of at least one misdemeanour. They ranged from tying a firework to a cat's tail when young to driving without insurance. Letting them talk amongst themselves for a while in a game of deviancy one-upmanship, he asked Prudence who had, as usual, been sitting silently, if she had ever committed a crime. Looking at that ingenuous expression, the word seemed inappropriate.

'When I was little,' she said quietly, looking him in the eye but rather distantly, 'I went to my uncle's farm and when I was walking around I found a yam on the ground that one of the pickers had left.' Her accent began to sound more African as she related the incident. 'There was nobody looking so I put it under my frock and took it home.' Looking briefly at the class she said, 'I don't know why I did it.' She looked back at him, again without expression.

'You should all be locked up,' he said, and began outlining the theories.

After he'd finished, having time for a quick coffee before his next lecture, he went to the refectory. She was standing outside.

'Can you see me alright now?'

'This time, yes.'

'I'm teasing. I shall have a tea, anyway.'

'I'll get it. Iced? Of course, they don't have iced tea over here.'

'Milk will do.'

It was quite crowded, but as he went to the counter she found a table in a corner. He bought her drink. 'You looked petty embarrassed when you gave your answer.'

'I was. You know; sometimes you and Mr. Lee seem on opposite sides.'

'Is it a competition?'

'It is in deterministic terms isn't it? You broach a topic one way, he another. I mean, he would say that psychologists adduce mental characteristics of individuals to explain social forms, while you would probably argue that these characteristics are themselves the result of the very social forms to be explained.'

'Does man make society or society make man? Isn't it good for discussion and debate?'

'Do we have to take sides?'

'Difficult not to see them as sort of clashing narratives, and we're tribal anyway.'

'We have metaphorical war paint and bones through our noses?'

'If you like.'

'I've seen war dances as a child. I don't want to see them again.'

He asked where she was last educated. It was the same college as her father in Pretoria, a private one; there was no tertiary education in her country.

'Look, I need to get this lecture ready, practice my spiel as they say.'

'That's Jewish, yes?'

CHAPTER FOUR

'Guess so.' He got up. 'See you whenever the next seminar is. For what it's worth, I think you'll do well here.'

She nodded. 'Bye then.'

As he left, he saw for a second some of the few teaching staff that were there looking at her. He hadn't noticed them or their looks while he'd been talking with her, perhaps they'd been saving them for when he was out of the door. On his way to the staffroom he tried to relate her to the few African Americans he knew. He couldn't. She was from a minority group of Africans with both education and money he'd never thought about the existence of; his childhood learning providing little more than pictures of natives, savages even, complete with loin cloths and joyously dancing to assorted percussion; another information vacuum in him. He recalled a quote from Ali Mazrui; 'You are not a country, Africa. You are a concept... a glimpse of the infinite.'

He didn't see her in his classes for the rest of the week, one of the pupils telling him he'd heard that she wasn't well. One evening Jess mentioned that there was a retirement party for one of the staff in the admin building in a couple of days and that she was going. He decided to go with her. He wasn't looking forward to it; something like this seemed to him a bit ordinary, having the potential to be rather depressing, even.

The first thing he really noticed as they entered the room, its desks, telex machines and typewriters pushed against its walls, was Prudence. She was in what looked like traditional African dress: long and red with some white 'V' shaped trimmings widening towards the bottom where it spread into a short train. She was talking with two lecturers, one a physicist he'd briefly met. For a moment he imagined her dancing in front of tribal elders and young men, floating, gliding then, as the drum rhythm grew more rapid and its noise louder, spinning and making almost frenzied movements, throwing her arms high and shaking herself; but not in that dress. For a second he had a flash of adolescent jealousy as he pictured the look in the eyes of the men.

Jess had stopped by a group of female staff. He caught her eye and pointed vaguely to where his student was and walked across to her.

'Hello.' he said casually, 'Hope you're not allowing these two to persuade you that science has all the answers.' He gave what he hoped was a bantering grin at them. 'Present them with this tautology: how we know what is in the world is determined by what is in the world and what is in the world is determined by how we know what is in the world. Just ask them to get outside of that.' He grinned again, feeling that it was a pretty inane one.

'This is rather inappropriate don't you think?' the older one said, frowning, 'It's supposed to be a party, is it not?'

'Yeh, I guess so. I'll leave you to it.'

'It's alright,' said his companion, 'we need to do some work. Nice to have met you, Miss.' As he turned away with his friend he said casually to him, 'The Physical sciences are the only proper subjects, are they not.'

Robert watched them move away. 'Jeez, that sounds so fuckin' English.' He could hear his Bronx return. He looked at her. 'Sorry, I shouldn't have said that, but it smacks of patronising the colonials. But, perhaps that's just my biased take.'

'Why did you say that stuff before? Was it a kind of battle? What or who over?' She was tightening her lips, her eyes smiling.

'How come you're here?'

'The Principal's Secretary invited me, I met her on the bus; we became friendly.'

'Somebody said you weren't well.'

'It's alright now; a woman's thing.'

He glanced at Jess. 'My wife's over there.'

As they moved towards Jess's group talking animatedly and loudly, he found himself cupping her elbow. Jess saw him and raised her eyebrows. He introduced them, feeling awkward, for a second there seemed an absence of appropriate norms. He looked from one to the other. Someone in the group was demanding Jess's attention and she turned back to them.

Robert guided Prudence away to where they'd been talking. She looked at him with a slight frown. 'You didn't tell me you were - '

'Should I have done? I guess you speak a few languages, uh?'

'You're changing the topic. I speak IsiZulu of course; it's a Bantu language, a little French and the English is coming along.'

Suddenly, he didn't want to talk about her background, he wanted to know how old she was, what time she went to bed, what time she woke to get to lectures, but instead asked her what her uncle grew on his farm.

'Mostly green maize, grapefruit, chicory roots sometimes. There's a village within the farm built around a cattle kraal. There's a sacred

CHAPTER FOUR

spot for worship and the girls, as you'd expect, assist their mothers while the boys herd the livestock.'

'The farm I'm living on is arable with a few cows, a bit like yours.'

'I doubt it, and why say, 'I am' and not 'we are?''

'Don't know. Why are you wearing that particular dress? It's fit for a palace.'

'Early socialization, Mr. Costain; formal dress for white man's parties.'

A fair haired girl came over to them and with a demanding grin asked Prudence where she'd been and to come over and talk to people. He guessed it was her new friend, perhaps her only one. The woman began dragging her away, asking if he minded. They went away, Prudence giving a quick look back at him.

He went to Jess's group and politely talked to them for a while before suggesting to his wife that as it was getting hot and stuffy, perhaps they should go outside for a stroll. She didn't wish to.

'You go if you want.'

He did, meandering about in the dusk looking at the flowers at the edges of the lawns and thinking of Prudence. He'd never expected to meet anyone like her or, really, meet anybody; he'd thought mainly of how to teach the pupils, thinking of them only in terms of how he could interest them in the subject, how he could help them. He remembered Norman telling him of a young lecturer he'd known who, he'd said, would refer to himself as a 'sociology lecherer' and who had, apparently, successfully played the field, saying that students demands could turn from academic to carnal in the space between two essays. 'He taught a thing called 'Sexual Divisions' and used to casually sit on the female students desks, smiling, encouraging, with a wink here, a studied frown there. He could strut sitting down.'

Robert could understand the temptation; power, as somebody said, could be an aphrodisiac. He went back; Jess was still talking with the group, some of whom had dispersed, and soon afterwards they left. She was quiet in the taxi home.

When they were back, she said, 'She seems a nice girl, very different. Is she bright?'

'Guess so. I'm still a bit hungry, have we anything?'

'Sure. Guess you can cook it yourself, Rob, I'm off to bed. G'night.'

This was a little unusual; mostly she would go to bed with or after him.

At his next lecture he wanted to push home the idea of reification, an abstract concept that seemed real and tangible, which he'd often thought was sociologically undervalued. He talked to them of the potency of ideas like duty and patriotism and their use by the establishment to defend their interests, especially in times of war, asking how many lives had been lost in their name throughout history. He'd looked meaningfully at a student slightly older than the others who had started the course late and who, on his first day, had worn a British Army captain's uniform, not wearing it again in college.

'Children are natural reifiers, how could they learn cultural values if they weren't'? And yes, society also is an abstract noun, but look how real it seems.' He made further references to the seductive force of patriotism as a national response to war, which, in the end, meant workers dying to defend the property of the rich.

'Am I being too simplistic to quote Marx and say that all war is class war? I could add to this, of course, by using the concept of objectifying people to turn then into objects of profit or, in war, of death.' Again a slightly lingering glance at the serviceman.

When he'd finished the captain came over to him and gave him a long, hard look.

'Well, I certainly don't agree with all you've said by a very long chalk, but I think that was the best damn lecture I've ever heard.' He put his hand out. 'Thank you.'

Robert shook it and the man walked away. He felt gratified, but also had a nudging awareness that it had been a bit of a performance; 'Look at me, clever me.' He walked towards the exit at the back of the theatre and saw Prudence alone in the hall, standing there.

'That was interesting. Do you want a coffee in the student bar?'

He told her it wasn't really for the staff and that she always seemed to be standing by doors.

'It's alright, it's on me and you're young enough to be studying here yourself and not everybody, believe it or not, knows who you are.'

The place was only sixty yards away; he let her get their coffees.

'Were you showing off?' she asked as she sat down. He shrugged.

'Why? Who were you attempting to impress? Yourself? Me?'

A part of him was aware that the answer was her.

CHAPTER FOUR

'I'll let you off the hook, that's one of your American sayings I think, and ask whether principles, reifications can get in the way of relationships.'

'They help make them don't they; vows, loyalty… '

She looked at him directly. 'Aren't they 'shoulds?'

'Of course.'

'And what of the personal?'

He thought it may have been a rhetorical question, but she stood and said, 'I have a class now. I shall be coming to your next one.' and before giving the smile again, said, 'And of course, we cannot derive an 'is' from an 'ought.''

He watched her leave, hurriedly yet gracefully casual. He noticed she'd hardly touched her coffee and also that some of the other students, too, were watching her as she disappeared around the corer of the Faculty building. He sat there wondering what she may have meant by the 'personal;' the imperatives that help bind people or, perhaps, that these things can obstruct personal feelings and, if so, for whom? He also mused on her parting line that something cannot be made from what we think it should be. Maybe she'd used it as a kind of reminder, but he wasn't certain of what. He also wasn't sure why he was giving it so much thought.

During the week before the Christmas holiday she didn't turn up to either his lectures or seminars, Norman casually telling him that the Principal's secretary had told him her friend had returned home to 'manage some family affairs,' not mentioning whether that meant London or Africa.

The holiday was a welcome break for Jess and it appeared to be for Norman also, but Robert missed the students and the stimulus almost as much as when he'd been off the campus at Reisler. There were just the three of them for the festive dinner; Norman's friend surprisingly choosing to stay in the Dordoigne despite the worry of the military build up on the Maginot line and the increasing threat of a Nazi invasion, while Doug, the farm foreman, who they'd invited, preferred to stay in his cottage. It was a pleasant occasion, but the unsettling aura of the 'phoney war' as Norman referred to it, seemed to be seeping into everything. He wondered where Prudence would be spending her Christmas.

The whole of the next term went by without a trace of her. There seemed no news of her, either. Rarely a day passed without him thinking of or being reminded of her as he sat teaching in his seminars or stood in the lecture theatre and lectured.

A few days before returning to academia after the Easter break, Robert, feeling the need for some urban pavements, persuaded Jess, who was increasingly settling into country life, to come to London for a day, wanting another attempt to get used to brown carriages, refreshment room tea urns, men pushing wheelbarrows, the trilbies and fox furs and the cornucopia of front doors. They travelled on the Underground, comparing it with the less attractive stations but more spacious trains on the Subway back home. He wanted to mooch around, she to shop. They compromised by going to Oxford Street and arranging to meet again in three hours while he took pot luck and got off at stations he liked the names of, getting out at Mansion House and Knightsbridge and, surprised by the flatness of the city, thinking of the impact the Chrysler Building would have made on the sensibilities of its inhabitants. Walking around Barons Court he went into a French run Victorian bakery and coffee shop, sat on its back terrace overlooking an overgrown, sparsely tombstone'd churchyard and tried to decide why he liked this place and its view so much. It was the sun. From his first visit on a damp, grey sky, leaf falling day, the city was now transformed. There was sun on trees, their tatty, black branches unnoticed for months suddenly becoming a green fusion of leaves overhanging mansard roofs, showing off an Italianate tower, shading a brightly lit window. It was so different from his home city, one of the few similarities being the brownstones in Brooklyn and on the Upper West Side; even a red brick Edwardian church, despite its stately sparseness, seemed to glow as he left the cafe and walked further along a street seeing, through the tops of trees, attic windows magicked by the sun. Jess had been waiting a while when he hurriedly walked up to her standing outside Selfrdge's.

Towards the end of the summer term she walked into his class.

'Sorry I'm late, have I missed much?' She sat at the end of the long table facing him, looking a little embarrassed. The dozen or so students sitting along the sides of the table looked briefly at her then back to him.

'Er, welcome back. We're discussing the man makes society, society makes man circularity which, I guess, we can't see any way out of.'

CHAPTER FOUR

For a while a few of them talked about it further, she contributing nothing and either looking down or at him. When they'd finished, some gave her polite smiles as they left.

'Have I missed much?'

'You mean this lesson or most of the two terms you've been absent?'

'I needed to go back home, my uncle died and my auntie was very sad. She is a real auntie. Children have lots of aunties in my country, they're really family friends. When I was a child and the teacher punished me for something and I met an auntie on my way home and told her why I was crying she would smack me for doing wrong, then when I got home my mother would also smack me for the same reason. It was strict. He was a politician. My father sent me to look at the will, to bring order to chaos, it is dealt with now. He owned a lot of land and as he had no children my father now has it. I wasn't sure what boat I would return on, if at all. At one time we were ready to sail then were taken off. When we did get a boat we didn't know until we were back that there were German U-boats about. I'm glad we didn't. What does sociology say about war?'

'It's an anomic situation, I suppose, a state of anomy, of normlessness, no behavioural guidelines.'

'Normlessness is the norm then.'

'That's kinda clever.'

'I hope I can make up the work. I will do the essays I've missed this year; my father has arranged it with the Principal.'

'We'll see. It's going to be a heck of a lot of work. I'll give you the titles now.' He went through his folder, wrote them quickly down and handed them to her.

'Thanks. I thought about you. I will go now and start work immediately.' She gave a perfect U.S. Army salute and went.

During the first part of the summer break, as well as occasionally visiting the university, Jess for some admin tasks and he using its disappointingly scant library, they helped the taciturn foreman and his part time labourers do odd jobs on the farm ranging from herding the few cows on it - Robert thinking back and finding it hard to believe he was actually doing this - putting up some fences, and jess learning to drive a tractor. Before the start of the academic year proper the university decided to begin a course for mature students who hadn't quite the required qualifications to begin an undergraduate course and those who wished to revise basic principles. The extra cash would be useful and Robert would rather be in the classroom than on the farm, anyway.

There were ten in the group, two of his own students; one of them Prudence. He went through some basics with them and set an essay, this time she leaving the classroom with the others. The following week he discussed their work, calling them individually to his desk to sit with him, leaving Prudence till last; partly looking forward to telling her that she'd earned the highest mark and, as she came towards his desk, knowing that mainly he wanted to feel her close to him. They were on their own. As she sat, she suddenly seemed to him to almost reek of privilege, to smell of a social class that was both alien and enviable. He was confused and tried to hide it by attempting humour, stretching his indigenous accent and saying, 'You may not believe this kid, but you is one fortunate dame, all those acres o' land pappy owns and him in Embassies and plush joints and the like hobnobbing with barons and earls and you gettin' an education and takin' it all for granted, uh?'

She looked surprised, started to laugh then stopped. 'Depends on your comparisons doesn't it? I think you've just told me what you feel about your background, but over here and in your country couldn't you argue that you're the privileged one, you're white aren't you?'

'Sure, in the States your brethren are -'

''Brethren?' where did that come from, rather biblical isn't it?'

He looked at her two feet from him, and said, 'You're an Oreo cookie.'

She frowned at him. 'What's that?

He looked at the large earring dangling from her ear knock against her cheek as she moved her head. He regretted saying it; it was cheap.

'Look, I'm sorry'

'What does it mean?'

'It's a slang term meaning someone who's black but is kind of white inside. It comes from -'

'Is that what you think?'

'No, of course not. I meant that you're... sophisticated, intelligent.'

'Not like my brethren then. Is that my fault, somehow? Do you want me to be collecting garbage in the Bowery or maybe shaking coconuts off a tree so that you can feel I'm genuine?'

CHAPTER FOUR

'Of course not, I'm...' He stopped himself; it seemed so ridiculous; sitting here with a student having this conversation.

She took her essay off his desk and stood, looking down at him.

'Isn't this an example of what principles do, this one being your confused ideology getting in the way?'

She walked towards the door and waved her essay. 'No need to go through this, I know it's good.' She turned. 'Incidentally, sophistication can mean snobbish and artificial. Am I that, then, am I not real, *Mister* Robert?'

She swung the door back hard as she left the classroom. He sat there, thinking of her yet again departing a room and leaving him muddled, but this time he wanted to go after her, walk down the stairs with her and try to explain himself. Not for the first time did he wish Billy was here.

When he got home it was Jess who told him they'd just heard that German bombs had been dropped on Coventry. Norman looked serious as they sat down to supper.

'It's occurred to me that there could be a lot more bombing and, if there is, it'll be on the capital.' He saw Jess's worried face. 'It shouldn't happen here, Jess, there'd be little point in going for anywhere in Norfolk, well, except Norwich and we're far enough away to be quite safe I should think.'

She asked where his parents were.

'In Winchester, fortunately they moved out of London some time ago. I stayed, of course, till Reisler. I'm letting my flat there as I may have told you. Incidentally, I haven't heard from Maurice yet, knowing him he's probably joined the Resistance. Keep your fingers crossed for him.'

'Why Coventry?' Robert asked.

'I don't know, maybe because it has, or perhaps had, a famous cathedral; a destruction of a symbol as a warning, the ultimate one being St. Pauls, of course. But whatever, it'll be London.'

'What about the children, they'll be... ' Jess looked down, shaking her head.

'Perhaps there'll be some sort of evacuation plan, move 'em to the country, maybe, who knows.' He was silent for a while. 'We could do something here couldn't we, if it happens? At least for a summer break, but your hands'll be full, Jess; you don't get the holidays we do.'

'*If* it happens.'

'Sure. They may only do a little damage before they're chased off, anyway, who knows, though we could make someone pretty comfortable. The child's parents will probably have visions of a farmer's wife, looking like a stout-armed advert for country goodness, cooking huge bowls of porridge and plates of eggs and teaching him to say 'White rabbits' on the first day of the month to bring him luck, that's what they say around here, while the farmer, wearing blue dungarees, wellies and a hat with straw sticking from it, will be leaning on a pitchfork looking wise and trustworthy.'

He chuckled, placed a forkful of food in his mouth, chewed for a while and asked Robert how his students were behaving.

CHAPTER 5

Holding a box camera in front of his face his father was telling him to keep still. He was standing in front of the shelter on their small oval lawn wearing a coat his aunt Gwen had made for him - he'd stood facing her with outstretched hands while she unravelled the wool by winding it around them - a puffed peak cap, gloves, white socks, some bedding strapped to his back, a gas mask in a cardboard box tied with a ribbon hanging from his shoulder and carrying a paper bag with some sandwiches in. Bluey was asleep by his shoe. His mother had also packed a small case with his clothes as well as his toothbrush and pyjamas; his identity card was in it also. He had heard her talking to aunt Flo months before about having him evacuated like many of the children in the area, but as there were no sirens or bombs then, had decided not to. His friends, like Alfie and the Bowhays, were still here.

Dad had to go to work so mum took him on the bus to Stratford station. Outside were policemen, people who worked at the station and lots of parents, though mostly children; he'd never seen so many all together. There were some teachers, too, though he never saw any from his own school. Lots of announcements came from loudspeakers and when somebody blew a whistle the station staff and policemen ushered the children inside and onto a platform. His mother took his cap off, spit on her fingers and slicked his hair down then put his cap back on and gave him a cuddle and a kiss before they were separated. He looked back to try to see her, but there were too many people. It was grey and noisy and he had to keep walking to the end of the platform.

'Come on, all aboard then,' shouted a man with a peak cap. 'Hurry yourselves, we ain't got all day.'

He climbed a step and squeezed into a carriage with other boys and girls who all wanted to get to the window. He tried pushing through to it, but couldn't get there. Some of them were waving; perhaps their parents had managed to get onto the platform. He was glad he'd said goodbye to Lenny. He'd kissed him on his cheek and was given a big, gummy grin and a punch on the face. He usually liked trains, especially when they started off and the steam hissed and blew out the chimney with long puffs which got shorter and shorter as they went faster, but this time he felt frightened. Mum had told him where he was going, but he'd forgotten what she'd said. He sat in a corner away from the window holding his case tightly; two of the bigger boys had thrown theirs up on the luggage rack, but he wanted to hold onto his. Although he was going away it would be okay, really, 'cos mum would ring him where he'd be staying either from the phone box in the Portway or from aunt Gwen's who had just got a phone.

He sat there squashed against a boy who smelt and was chewing gum and showing his yellow teeth. He looked down at his shoes that dad had cleaned, which he called 'buffing' because he'd been in the army. They stopped at a big station which had even more people and noise. Somebody, he thought it may have been one of he teachers, put a hand on his back when he got off the train and guided him away from the others and, with two girls walking next to them, went to the barriers and then to a platform where there was another train waiting. He felt a bit of a sissy walking with the girls. He looked quickly down to make sure he still had the label with his name and address on tied to his collar, though he wasn't sure why it was there because he knew where he bloody lived; he saw dad in his mind when he said 'bloody.' He got to the window this time because here were only the two girls and the teacher in the carriage. He sat by it, looking out and not speaking till they said goodbye to him at Colchester and the teacher told him that he was going on to Norwich where he would be met.

He'd never seen so much space and grass and trees. It was bigger than Barking Park and there were no railings. It stretched everywhere; it was like going to Canvey, but further away and the sky was bigger. He could see ploughed earth and hedges and ponies and cows; he didn't remember seeing a cow before and wondered what it would be like to get close to one. Alfie had told him that the milk bottles left on door steps were cow's eggs; he didn't know whether he meant it or not. And there were black barns, straw and farmhouses.

When the train stopped he didn't want to get off, it was warm and safe and he liked looking out the window, especially when the train was moving. He didn't want to go where he was going, he wanted to keep on the train and ride on and on looking at the clouds and bits of sky. He put his head outside the window and saw other children getting out of the carriages and onto the platform. He couldn't understand why he'd been left on his own while the others seemed to

CHAPTER FIVE

be together and with teachers taking them towards the start of the platform. He stepped down and walked behind them into the big space past the ticket barrier. They all stood about till the people who were waiting there went across to the children and began talking to them and taking them away with them, they seemed to be choosing the boys and girls they liked best. He hadn't really thought about it, had taken it for granted that his mother and father knew who he would be staying with, but they didn't. He watched the other kids, one by one, sometimes in twos, go off with the adults until he seemed to be the only one left.

There were a few policemen there, but they were going now so he stood still holding his case and sandwiches. Then a lady and two men came towards him, a broad man with a trilby hat who looked like a boxer, a tall man who was clean shaven, his mum liked that in a man she'd say, as long as he wasn't fair haired, she liked dark men, and a lady who said, 'Hi.' to him in a strange accent and bent and looked at the label around his neck.

'It's Keith, is it? Hello.' She shook his hand; nobody had shaken his hand before. 'Sorry we're late, it's our fault; do you want to come with us?'

He didn't say anything. The tall man took the case from him and they went outside. He wondered if they'd taken him because there were no more children left. They told him their names, but he knew he wouldn't remember them right away. The boxer looking man asked if he'd enjoyed his journey. He nodded; he felt shy. They went out of the station to a car. Norman, he remembered his name now, said he could sit in the front if he wanted. He'd only been in a car once, a taxi, when dad had taken them for a supper at a big pub near where uncle Harry worked. As they started, the lady, Jess, touched his shoulder and said, 'We'll contact your parents right away so they know where you are.' He nodded again.

They'd been driving a while and he was watching the fields and cottages and farms go past.

'A bit different from London, uh?' the tall man asked him. He spoke like Jess.

'Leave him alone, he's just got here,' he heard her whisper. He wondered if there would be snow, a lot of Christmas cards showed snow. He'd just drawn a Christmas card for mum and dad of a snowman with a piece of shrapnel for his nose and a soldier's tin hat on, and one for Lenny with Mickey Mouse on the front and Goofy on the inside.

They turned into a long, narrow lane at the side of a field and a big house at the end of it with a tall chimney on one side and lots of panes in the windows. There was a roof like a castle and under another window vegetables were growing like on the allotments over the park before they'd put the big gun on them. When the car stopped and they got out, Norman said, 'Well, this is it, Keith, welcome to Heath Park.' Jess told him that was the name of the house. Aunt Doll had a piece of wood with 'Charldorn' outside her house; mum said it was Charlie and Doll's names put together.

It was the biggest kitchen he'd ever seen; the ceiling had wooden beams holding it up which reminded him of a palace in a film he and mum had seen about Henry The Eighth, a huge cooker and pots and pans hanging on the wall.

Jess asked him if he was hungry. 'We're eating together this evening and managed to get some steak. That okay?'

He didn't think he'd had steak before. 'Yes, please,' he said. It was the first time he'd spoken since he'd met them. He enjoyed the meat and liked sitting with them; there was a fire in the room and they talked to one another and smiled at him without making him say anything. They had apple dumpling for afters, which they called dessert, then Jess asked him if he was tired.

'Shall I show you where your bed is?'

He followed her up the stairs where she took him in the room next to hers and Robert's and said goodnight to him. Someone had already put his case and gas mask in it and there was a small sink in the corner. He'd never seen a bedroom with a sink in. He cleaned his teeth, lay under the patchwork quilt which looked like tiny square fields with hedges around them and thought of the way the people spoke. Norman was posh, but he'd heard people speak like Robert and Jess in a film at the Broadway when aunt Flo had let him and Terry Bowhay in for nothing. He pulled the quilt over him and wondered what his mother and Lenny were doing.

'What d'you think then?' Robert asked when Jess came back into the room.

'Don't know, really, he seems pretty unsure doesn't he, but then you'd expect it. He's not very big is he, dear little face though, brown eyes and tiny ears. I think I'm gonna like him.'

CHAPTER FIVE

'As we've discussed,' said Norman, he needs to carry on his formal education, pity he can't go to the school here, but unless between us we can take him and pick him up regularly... ' He shrugged. 'We can't keep asking people to fill in for us at college or your place. Not sure what he knows, but I have a feeling he's up to scratch.'

'You make him sound like a racehorse,' Jess said.

'And why the bedding, do they think he's going camping? And what do you think of that gas mask, what are they expecting? It's like something out of the last war. Look, I'm off; I need to write some notes to myself for tomorrow. We'll try to make him happy, eh? He'll be alright. Goodnight to you two.' He left the room.

The knocking on his door sounded different; it was a gentle tapping. The curtains were different, too, they were a brown colour and there was light coming in at the sides, there was no black-out at the window and no wallpaper, the walls were cream and plain and the door wasn't painted, it was varnished wood.

'Keith?'

It wasn't mum's voice; it was the lady with the funny accent. She spoke his name again. 'It's Jess. Remember?'

'Shall I get up?'

'I think you should; have some breakfast.'

He saw his towel hanging over the sink; he didn't have to go through to the scullery to wash. He dressed and opened the door. She was standing on the landing and asked him if he'd slept well. She ushered him down the stairs and asked what he usually had for breakfast. He told her.

'Well, we don't have much porridge in the States, but we do have some here, it's mostly Norman's, and is it bread fried on both sides?'

'Yes, please'.

'Okay, sit yourself down.'

He ate his food and tried to drink some coffee, but it was too strong tasting, not like the stuff they had at home.

'You do like your tea, you English, uh?'

He nodded. She told him she wouldn't always be giving him his breakfast, it depended on who of them had to go to work and when.

'That okay?' He nodded again.

The white tablecloth was like his mum's which he sometimes helped her shake the crumbs off in the garden, she holding one end and he the other, both spreading their arms and moving them quickly up and down, like when they folded the sheets she'd taken off the line, he walking towards her holding his end then she folding them and giving them to him to carry indoors, telling him not to fall over or she'd have to wash them again.

When they'd finished breakfast Jess suggested she show him some of the farm. He went upstairs for his coat and they went out into the yard. There was a kind of stable place with cows and smells and lots of straw on the ground; he hadn't realised how big they were. They were brown and white like some of the horses in cowboy films. There was a boy on a stool by the side of one pulling on its udders. He looked up at them and stared at Keith. Jess told him the boy's name was Jamie, who sometimes did the milking and was the nephew of the farm foreman. He was as big as Alfie.

'You'll be seeing each other, I dare say.' She looked down at him, 'I think you should call your parents, tell them you've arrived. Norman has already I think, or should have.'

He went back into the house, took off the wellingtons she'd given him and went upstairs to look for aunt Gwen's number on his identity card which he'd shown to Norman. The phone was on a small table in the hall next to the stairs. She asked him if he wanted to dial the number. He rang and held the phone to his ear. He heard the dialling tone and Aunt Gwen saying hello. He didn't say anything.

'Say something,' said Jess, 'speak up.'

'Is that you, Keith?' He nodded and told her it was.

'Is it nice there? Is it a big farm? Are the people nice?' D'you want to speak to your mum, she's coming round later; if you want, she'll call about six, that alright?'

He looked at Jess; she nodded.

'Yes.' He gave the phone back to her and she spoke into it for a while.

They went outside again, walked to the barn which was a big black one then to a field with a narrow stream at the bottom where he asked if it had any tiddlers or sticklebacks in; she didn't know what he meant. He told her what they were and that he used to fish for them with a net on the end of a cane in the stream at the back of aunt Doll's house and that he'd always throw them back after catching them. As it started getting dark he saw some sheep huddled in a

CHAPTER FIVE

corner of a field near a hedge and they went back to the farmhouse to get warm.

Just after he heard Norman's car coming up the drive, Jess called him out to the phone. Mum's voice asked him if he was alright and after he told her he was there was a silence. 'What's it like on a farm then, lots of cows? Enjoying your food?'

'Yes.'

'Lenny's asleep.'

He heard a whisper then, 'I'll put you through to Gwen. You can write to me.'

Aunt Gwen asked him how the train journey was then told him to give the phone to the lady who'd answered.

Jess said, 'Yes, he's fine,' and laughed. 'Yep, porridge and fried bread. Sure, I'll tell him.' She replaced the phone and told him his aunt would send him some sweets.

'Was it nice to hear from your mum?'

He didn't really know. He wondered what he was doing here and thought of Lenny asleep in his cot.

She was at his next lecture, sitting at the back, expressionless. It put him off a little, forgetting momentarily the beginning of what he'd worked on the night before when he'd casually asked Keith if he'd like him to read to him, being a little surprised when he'd said yes. A quick thought was that either he'd been used to being read to and wanted a familiar comfort or it had rarely occurred. He began his talk and continued as planned, noticing her taking copious notes. When he'd finished, knowing that he had planned a little too well, it was rather mechanical and stifling, he slowly put his notes together, looked up and saw her standing directly in front of him while the rest of them filed out. There was no teasing smile or that slight lean of her head, just a faintly challenging look. He asked her if she wanted to see him about something. Still looking directly at him she said that she wasn't sure, but perhaps they could talk over coffee. He felt slightly apprehensive as he said yes.

'Are you surprised that I want to talk to you?'

'Yes.'

'So am I, but an apology would suffice.'

'Let me explain, I -'

She looked at him directly again

'Okay, I apologise, but -'

'That'll do.'

Again they sat in the corner of the refectory; he was aware of the other occupants deliberately not looking at them.

She flicked her earring. 'It's my birthday, I'm having a party; do you wish to come?'

'Today?'

'No. Thursday. You look doubtful. It's a legitimate request.' She still hadn't given him that teasing smile.

'On my own?'

'Yes, as my teacher. I may give you an apple if you're good.'

'Who'll be there?'

'We'll have to see.' She held out a slip of paper. 'The address.'

She bent her head to glance at his watch. 'Hell, I have a class with Norman Lee.' She got up hurriedly. 'About eight. See you.'

She went out. Neither of them had bought coffee.

Staying to see a student who was struggling with the subject and who he had advised several times to change it but was obdurately holding on, he returned to the house after their evacuee had gone to bed. Norman was just leaving the table as he came into the room and, after the usual greeting, noticed a half completed IQ test paper on a dining chair.

'Bored, Norman? I didn't think you thought much of the validity of these things.'

'I don't, I was using it in a seminar to point out the problems of measuring what we call intelligence, trying to quantify the qualitative, if you like.'

Jess came in with food. 'If you're talking about that test thing, it was Keith, he did it while I was cooking; sometimes I think he'd sooner do something like that than talk.'

Both Robert and Norman reached for it at the same time, bumping their heads.

'Irony,' Jess murmured, 'irony.'

They looked at it. 'He's good,' Norman said. 'You obviously can learn to do well at these tests, but I doubt whether he's had the opportunity, especially in one so young. How old is he, eleven?'

'I think so,' said Jess, joining them.

'His progressive matrices and verbal comprehension are excellent. Most of the adults I know, especially at university,' he smirked, 'couldn't do as well. How long did it take him?'

CHAPTER FIVE

'Dunno, about half an hour or so. What you're saying is, he's bright, yes?'

'Very. Interesting here is that the currently fashionable biological inheritability of IQ probably doesn't count for much nor, assuming his parents are manual workers, do social class factors.'

Jess looked at them both. 'I've got a letter here that may interest you.'

She went to the dresser and picked up an envelope. 'He wrote it to his parents this afternoon and gave it to me to post. I opened it. I thought it wise in case he was telling them about something he didn't like here. It's a bit strange, the words he uses. He kind of describes things, but there's little about people, about us. Somehow, he doesn't seem to be writing to them either. It's like a school essay or something. I was going to post it in the morning, but if you want to look at it you can.' She handed the letter to her husband.

He opened the envelope. 'Well, it starts off conventionally enough, 'Dear mum and dad,' then it's all description, adjectives, as if he doesn't know what to say to them, it's like a stream of visual consciousness, 'Moonbeams lighting the roof of the edifice, the dust swirling in the light.' Probably looking out of his window at night. Where did he get 'edifice' from? And this, 'It was like a subterranean tunnel with a baby tumbling through it and above was an airplane slowly spiralling down from a bright red sky over the houses, the screaming pilot hanging from its wheels.' Then he ends with, 'Hope you are well, and Lenny.' Who's Lenny?'

'I think it's his little brother,' said Jess.

He handed it to Norman who quickly read it. 'He has a rather bizarre imagination as well as quite a vocabulary; the war's affected him, also. He's interesting.'

'What as, Norman?' she asked, 'some sort of object to analyse or a boy we've volunteered to look after?'

He frowned. 'Of course we're looking after him, Jess, these are merely... bits of academe, detached bits and pieces we're interested in.'

He turned to Robert. 'I'm giving a lecture next week on Piaget's biological model of intellectual development, can you make it?'

Having missed his previous one at Reisler, Robert said he would. But what interested him more was that he knew so little about this child.

To dilute the lie of having to go into town to privately tutor some students, he stayed after a seminar with two of the older ones who, though their continuous assessment work was competent, their exam technique wasn't. Prudence had left a note in his pigeon hole that morning saying that before he came to the party they could meet in a restaurant in Norwich; he wasn't sure why she would want this. Norman had lent him his car with a rather firm reminder that, 'Here we drive on the left.' He idly wondered why she hadn't asked her senior lecturer.

He arrived before her. It was a dismal place; flock wallpaper, match boarded dado, eclectic period furniture and a tattered, misspelt notice stating that there were rooms to let. It was more like a run down bar than a restaurant, almost Bronx-like. She came in wearing a well cut jacket and skirt that made the place look even more inappropriate for her. She sat opposite him at a table

'Why here?'

'I wanted to know if you were happy to be seen with me in public, not at the university, but here. Incidentally, there seems to be a growing disappointment around that your country's not helping in the war. Guess I'm the wrong colour and you're the wrong nationality.'

'You haven't been here before, have you.'

'No, one of the students said it was okay.'

'It looks the kinda place where the landlady would say that she couldn't shake your hand 'cos she'd just finished putting lard on the cat's boil.'

She looked momentarily bemused then said, 'You know we're being looked at, don't you. Do you think they assume I've escaped from a circus?'

He looked around him; there weren't many people and most flicked their eyes away from her as he did so.

'Am I a sex object now?''

'If they're thinking that, does it matter?' D'you want a drink or are we going to your party?'

She got up, asked him if he had a car then told him to follow hers and that she lived nearby. They parked outside a large Victorian house two streets away.

'This is different from the other boarding house; I live in the upstairs flat here.'

CHAPTER FIVE

She opened the large, ornate front door and they walked up the narrow stairs to the landing.

'It seems pretty quiet for a party.'

She went into a room at the end of the landing, holding the door open for him.

'Come in.'

It was a large room with a high ceiling, a picture rail from which hung pictures of lions and hills, sunsets and dawns and a painting, full of sensual, sentimentalised Victorian sexuality, of a young girl lying on her back in a bed of white roses, another girl by her side about to kiss her watched by a curly haired boy peeking from a bush. There was also, beside the fireplace, a half-sized *papier mache* lion. But there were no people.

'Are we early or something?'

'No, it's just you and me.'

'What about your friend, the one who works for the Principal, isn't she coming? '

'We're going out tomorrow, I wanted you here today. Stop frowning. I have a malt whiskey here, I don't know whether you drink it, but relax anyway, sit down.'

While he did she went toward a small drinks cabinet and poured two glasses. She gave one to him and sat on a pouffe opposite him.

He gestured around him. 'Is this all your stuff here?'

'Of course.'

'Somehow, I was expecting something religious.'

With her Nefertiti head inquiringly angled she said, 'Why, because I'm African? How many times have you told us of social inequality being divinely legitimised by hymnal lines such as, 'The rich man at his castle, the poor man at his gate, all creatures high and lowly, God ordered their estate?' You know I'm aware of this, anyway, and though I do go to church with my father sometimes, it was a rather silly thing to say.' She paused for a while. 'What I was trying to tell you the other day was that although you feel you should love your wife, you can't make it an 'is'.'

She seemed remarkably grown up. He wished he did.

'She's too ordinary for you; I don't care how nice a person she is, generous, honest or whatever. I'm here now, in front of you. Look at me.'

He did, she was just sitting there, her posture could have been a man's, but she was so female. He had no idea why, but the situation reminded him of what he'd been idly thinking of late, of the primitive in humanity and if there could be a society to optimise that nature, to fulfil itself, but of course, given the power of the id... '

'You're intellectualizing again, I can feel it. 'What are you running away from?'

'I'm sorry. I need to go.' He stood.

'Need to, or feel you *have* to? More duty, Robert?'

As he went out of the room and down the stairs he remembered in his final week at Reisler an auburn haired girl in the library asking him to come for a celebratory drink she and her friends were having that evening. He'd said no and, as he watched her drive off looking back out of the side window, he'd walked to the bus stop intermittently kicking his calf to berate himself for a missed opportunity. He crossed the hall and opened the door wondering if he hadn't stayed because of what he felt for Jess or, as Prudence had suggested, a principle. As he walked down the front steps and into the car he realised he hadn't wished her a happy birthday.

He went to Norman Lee's lecture on Piaget, the days before it divided into teaching, thinking of Prudence and talking to Keith. He was a quiet child, but had flashes of what Norman called cockney humour; he seemed quick witted and tended to read quite a lot. Having a free morning he'd taken him to the village library where he chose books, one of which Robert thought a sixteen year old may read. He didn't say much; just mentioning how quiet it was in the country and how few people there seemed to be. He asked if the foreman's nephew was still living in the cottage, Robert assuming that he needed someone around his own age to play with.

'I'm not sure, but I can find out. Missing your mates?'

He nodded again. In reply to his telling, at Robert's request, what sort of games he played with them, the latter told him about the sort of things he did at the same age: model trains, Lincoln logs which he built castles and buildings with, Crayola crayons and baseball.

'We had marbles and played kick the can like you, but I've an idea I'd have enjoyed myself more with knock down ginger, uh? Perhaps I would have broken fewer windows, too.' He smiled down at him and got a grin in return.

'I used to have crayons,' Keith said, 'but use pencils now and Indian ink as well, mostly for details. I've a pen with a tiny nib my aunt Gwen bought me; it's called a mapping quill.'

CHAPTER FIVE

Robert asked him what he liked to draw. By the time he'd finished answering, he appeared to be less shy, almost animated.

'Wanna draw something for me when we get back; anything you like.'

When they returned and after cajoling him out of his room, Robert, sitting opposite him at the dining table, watched him draw a racehorse and a World War 1 tank then asked him if he ever copied drawings or photos. When he received an affirmative nod he asked him to draw something he'd recently copied. Asking for another piece of paper he began. After a completely silent hour in which Robert a little disinterestedly mapped out a forthcoming lecture, he walked around the table and bent over the boy's shoulders. It was a very detailed sketch of a tomb with inscriptions and miniature heads on each corner, and it was obvious that anyone of his age wouldn't have possessed the required level of draughtsmanship to have drawn the original. It was a copy and he'd remembered, probably, every line.

Jess came in, started cooking a meal and asked what they'd been doing.

'This and that,' said Robert.

'It was good,' said Keith quietly, looking across at him.

The lecture's title was, 'The Biological Process of The Evolutionary Adaptation of The Species.' and Norman delivered it well, most of the students and staff there taking notes.

Robert took the bus home as usual, Jess arriving just after him, Keith was with Jamie at his uncle's cottage where he would be fed before being brought back. Norman walked into the kitchen.

'Don't know how long you've been here, but I expect I could have given both of you a lift back, I thought I'd have to stay a lot longer. What did you think of it then?' he asked Robert. They went into the long room and sat at the table.

'Yeh, so Piaget observed his children not only assimilating objects to fit their needs, but also modifying some of their mental structures to meet the demands of new objects, their changing environment if you like.'

'Yes, assimilation and accommodation; the need to balance the two triggering intellectual growth.'

'I was thinking of Keith and thought that perhaps a child could not only modify what's there, a schema, as you call it, but actually create a new one.'

'I suppose it's possible, but why would he do that?'

'Because, maybe, what's already there is so painful, perhaps it's nearly always been there and could be a kind of emotional brutalising, especially from his father. I'm guessing this of course, but you did tell us to be intuitive, remember?'

'Indeed.' Norman looked towards the kitchen. 'I think you should sit in on this, Jess, you see him as much as anyone.'

She stood in the doorway. 'Not if you're gonna make with the words, boys, he's a child, not an object of investigation. Anyway, I'm mostly his cook, you're his mentors, Rob tends to be with him when he's drawing; he reads to him, too.'

'I think,' said her husband, 'he probably learnt to read almost entirely at school and through his own interest.'

'He does look kinda scared at times,' said Jess, 'but his eyes don't really show it, they're -'

'Impassive?' asked Norman.

'Yes, as if he purposely dulls them, his mouth's a tight little line.'

'We think, or Robert seems to,' said Norman, 'that there are problems, how far back they go, who knows. We'd like to help, though Rob has more opportunity than me, as indeed, you have, I'm either out or at home and occupied, as you know; this job's a little more than I bargained for. Continue, Robert.'

'Okay, this new schema, if there is one, could be a fantasy world, a world of words, of things: shapes, spaces, buildings, things he gets emotional atmospheres from, if you like; look at the letter he wrote. He's done this to survive an alienation from, I think, his parents, especially his father, thus from the world, perhaps. In Piaget's terms, these elemental structures have been damaged. In short, he cannot accommodate the external world unless he changes it into a fantasy one, or part fantasy.'

'Why do you suggest this is what Keith may have done? And why the father?'

'Simply because he never mentions him. '

From the kitchen Jess said, 'That bit's probably the only part I've really understood so far, but it's true he doesn't mention his dad, well I've never heard him.'

'Me neither, his mother, yes, and there's an aunt Gwen, a Flo and a boy called Alfie, I think, that's about it. You seem pretty sure of your theory, Robert.'

'Maybe it's misguided empathy, but it's what I feel.'

CHAPTER FIVE

'Don't you think you could be exaggerating all this? You know a little of Piaget and, it could be argued, only a little more about the boy, and you're projecting it onto him, perhaps because he's the only child you know. You like him, you think he has problems, you want to help him. I understand that, but there's no convert like the new convert, we tend to use theory like crutches sometimes: Marx, Wittgenstein, shove Jesus in there if you like, but let's not get too -'

'Look, you know more about this sort of stuff than me, but he covers it up, lives through it, he survives. You could argue that his intellectual growth has been accelerated by there being little else *but* that part of him; to an extent he kinda *becomes* the external world, well part of him does.'

Norman was quiet for a while, looking at Robert, 'You know, if what you say is true or even partly so and the significant relationship, or non-relationship, is with the father then I don't see how we can really help him, it's too deep, too primary.'

'That's probably what I think, too.'

'I think you're also hinting that emotionally he's even younger than he is; maybe a three year old?'

Jess came back into the room. 'I want to show you something.' She hurried upstairs and came down holding two sheets of lined paper from an exercise book. 'I was cleaning his room and saw this. I forgot to put it back.'

Norman took them from her and he and Robert read them. There were detailed descriptions of his room, the kitchen, the room they were in and the coloured glass window at the top of the stairs; also described was the dust on the bottom segment of a door panel and the colours of the carpet patterns.

'It's so detailed,' said Robert, 'like some of his drawings; he really sees things doesn't he, he does with his sketches, as if he's standing right in front of whatever he's drawing. And this thing at the end, 'I love the gurgling freedom of drinking straight from a Tizer bottle.' How many kids his age phrase like that?'

Jess put their meals on the table where they ate mostly silently; Robert thinking, between imagining Keith looking intently around his room as he wrote, of the three essays Prudence had recently put in his pigeon hole. He hadn't seen her for a week. He'd read them in the refectory; it was as if she was with him. They were critical, not only of the expected theoretical perspectives to be used as answers, but of the questions themselves.

Having had the idea in his mind for a few weeks, Robert decided he would go to London and see Keith's parents at mid-term. Jess was needed at work for most of that week, but Norman would be around more and Doug's nephew was back with him for a while and was occasionally seeing Keith; they were, to Robert's mild surprise, getting on well, though were two very different children. He had seen another drawing, the word 'antidisestablishmentarianism' writ large across the top and underneath two boys pointing up, one saying, 'What, swallowed a dictionary?' and the other, 'We had one, but the wheels come off.' He assumed this had been typical schoolboy reactions to Keith's vocabulary. He asked Jess if she'd have come with him if she was able.

'I'm not sure.' I'm okay here.'

'But, you like London, especially the first time we were there.'

'Yeh, that was then.'

He couldn't understand the meaning, if any, of the reply.

He wrote to them, the mother replying. She would obviously like to see her son, but understood that it was best he stay where he was while the bombing continued and to give Keith her love. He himself would be most welcome, but there was, unfortunately, no room for him to stay. It was neatly written, the phrasing stilted. He told himself to stop trying to be a graphologist and to accept it as it was.

'Are you going to tell the boy you're going?' Jess asked.

'I think so, it may upset him, but it's still dangerous there, they've had over five months of it, it's been relentless, apparently.'

When he told Norman, he reminded him that it was the child's perception that counted, not his. 'Logic isn't always the best guide here. Try to remember that.'

'I'm not going just for that, I would like to reassure them that their son's okay.'

'But, while you're there?'

'Okay, it'd be an interesting background to a case study, if you like, we'll see; they're probably quite ordinary, respectable people.'

'Nobody's quite as respectable as the respectable English working class.'

Jess had heard them. As Norman went to his room, she said, 'He's talking sense, forget theory, he's a child, a person, not something to pick apart.'

CHAPTER FIVE

'Of course, but theory can help; we use accepted theory all the time; you pour a coffee based on the theory of gravity being true, you -'

'Okay, mister clever, but don't hurt him.' She looked determined; her eyes almost held a warning. This wasn't the easy going, understanding Jess that he'd married.

CHAPTER 6

He began to see the damage the nearer he got to the city: gaps between thirties houses in the suburbs, larger ones in the terraced streets of east London, a park with flattened trees and two large craters and, as he began walking downhill from Plaistow station, a wide area of debris in front of him just south of the address he'd been given. It all seemed so miserable: the cars, the people's clothes, two pubs, one of them closed, a row of grey shops and shabby lines of Victorian houses all lit, still, by turn-of-the century pavement lamps, with children playing soccer under one of them with a bald tennis ball. He looked in a grocer's shop where a man behind the counter was cutting cheese with a wire while women were queuing outside, some holding ration books; it seemed much easier for Jess to get food. The debris looked even bigger as he walked along the edge of it. There was a frame of a bicycle like an isosceles triangle sticking up from a small lake of mud surrounded by bricks and lumps of concrete and wood, but generally it had been flattened and cleared of any large parts of buildings that had been left standing, though there were two houses next to each other that seemed virtually intact. He tried not to imagine what had been there and what had happened. He wanted to see St. Paul's, the Palace, the Abbey and maybe a couple more tourist traps, if they were still there, but for now it was the boy's parents.

The woman who came to the door was tall with hair that seemed a little too dark for her face. She held out her hand. 'Pleased to meet you I'm sure,' she said, holding the door open for him.

He wiped his feet on the mat behind it and followed her through to a room at the end of the narrow passage. A man of average height and build with a square chin and wearing a pullover was sitting with his back to him at a table.

'Fred, this is Mister Costain.'

'Yeh, I suppose it is, 'ello mate,' he said, half rising from his chair then sat down again as if wanting to get back to his newspaper.

'Do sit down,' his wife said, 'have my chair, I'll get you something. What would you like?'

'Well, that's nice of you. Coffee would be fine.'

CHAPTER SIX

'Afraid we don't drink much of that Mister Costain, we have 'Camp,' sort of imitation coffee, really. Will tea do?'

'That'll be fine, also, and call me Robert, please.'

She went into the tiny kitchen. He felt cramped, almost claustrophobic amongst the winged victory ornaments on the mantelpiece above the black grate and the flower patterned wallpaper and carpet.

'So, you're American, eh?'

'Guess so, Mister Clements.'

'Where you from then?'

'New York, the Bronx.'

'eard o' that, it's a neighbourhood an' it? Never been there meself. 'spect there'll be more of you over 'ere eventually 'elpin' us win the war.'

'Couldn't tell you about that.'

She came in with a thatched cottage teapot, placed it on the table and went back for some cups and saucers. 'D'you want a cup, Fred?' she asked from the kitchen.

He grunted. As she poured she asked her visitor whether her son was alright.

'Yes, he's fine, we like him; I hope he likes us, I think he does.'

'It's really nice of you to come all this way to tell us.'

'Not annoying you is he, with his drawings and stuff?' asked her husband. 'Too much of it if you ask me.'

'On the contrary, it pleases us. He draws well and he's bright too.'

'You can be too bright, you know, it can turn people off yer.'

'Is he eating well?' she asked.

'Very, he does like his porridge and fried bread.'

She smiled, 'Good, he's eating, that's everything.'

'Play football over there do they?' her husband asked.

'A little bit, it's called soccer.'

He grunted again.

She asked if he was hungry. He told her he'd eaten on the train.

'We haven't got much, but you're welcome to it.'

He'd bought some food. He opened his duffel bag and handed her steaks, a few pounds of carrots and some eggs. He gave her a Hershey bar. 'I bought a few of these over in case I felt homesick.'

Her eyes lit up when she saw the steaks. 'Are you sure? It really is kind of you, really.'

'It's okay, I know you're having a tough time and it's easier for us in the country.' He looked at her husband and thought he saw a brief glimpse of envy, a look that may have said, 'They come over here, eat our food, get more of it than us then… ' He decided he'd probably imagined it. He saw him look at his watch then stand, brushing non-existent crumbs from his pullover. He turned to Robert.

'Time to go now, another night shift, but I won't get any kip. It's a pity you can't be here a bit longer, I'm goin' to the British Legion tomorrow, go most Saturdays lately, or when I can, that is. You'd like it, we play Al Bowlly records quite a bit, he's just died o' course, and Paul Robeson, though I don't hold with his politics, mind yer. Anyway, I got to go. Hope its quiet tonight for yer. Cheerio.'

He put on his raincoat and cap and left, Robert feeling that he didn't really want him joining him at his club and hadn't been keen on meeting him anyway. Mrs. Clements asked some more questions about her son which he answered as truthfully as he could then, as dusk began and feeling he wouldn't find out much more of any significance, told her he would go, too.

'I think you'd better, we might get a heavy one tonight.'

He asked her what had happened at the debris and if it had affected the house.

'It was a bomb, a big one; we had to have some plastering done on two of the ceilings and this window was blown clean out,' she gestured towards it, 'but the war damage people came and fixed it, they were pretty quick about it.'

'He seems a nice guy, your man.'

She hesitated. 'Well, he's a good provider, always has been, and never laid a hand on Keith. His dad used to hit him a lot, that's why he run away and joined the army in India, to get away from him. No, he don't like physical contact does Fred. He hardly touches Keith, hope he's not going to be like that with Lenny, that's Keith's little brother, he's asleep at the minute.'

Again, it may have been a function of his imagination, but he thought there was a momentary bitterness in her eyes.

'Anyway, never mind all that, is the schooling okay, well, what you're teaching him, that is.'

'Sure, we've seen the local school programme and we kinda take turns, a bit of this and that; history maths, geography, English, he needs very little help with that, don't worry.'

CHAPTER SIX

'I'm not, I know he's in good hands with you and your wife, especially now I've met you.'

'He doesn't speak about your husband much.'

'Well, it gets strained between them sometimes, he does his duty though; takes him to London sometimes, buys toys and things when he can, you know.' She was quiet for a moment. 'When Keith rang the other evening we were at my sister's and Fred picked it up and said, 'Clements here.' as if he was at work or still in the army. 'Want to speak to your mother, son?' She forced a grin. 'I wanted him to go to Essex, but Fred thought it was too near London. Ne'er mind, he's with you now.' There was a sound upstairs. 'That's Lenny awake.'

'I better be going Mrs. Clements, find my hotel and so forth.'

He told her he admired her courage and resilience and would think of them when he heard there'd been another raid on the city. She thanked him for coming and held her hand as if to squeeze his arm, then stopped herself. He waved to her at the gate. She smiled and closed the door.

As he walked by the side of the debris back towards the station he thought of the husband. He seemed principled, but unimaginative, unaware, lacking empathy. As the word 'duty' came back he thought of Prudence and her reifications; she would have had a field day, he was, seemingly, full of them, 'Filling the space where real relationships should be,' she'd say. He hadn't once asked after his son. He tried to imagine what it must be like for him when, returning from work, he saw, across the Thames, the flashing sky, not knowing if there were incendiary'd streets under it, his home no longer there.

He went to Buckingham Palace on the Tube, as Norman called it. The trains seemed to be about the only thing here that was more up to date than in New York, most of them looked a little more modern than the ones at home that went to Queens and Coney Island, with rivets all over the outside and hard benches inside. There were sandbags piled around the base of the building and at the side of the sentries and Horse Guards at the gate and he was rather disappointed at the design and size of the place. He'd noticed the same somewhat fragile protection around a few of the public buildings he'd passed on the way. He went on the Tube again, checked into his hotel, a rather scruffy one off Tottenham Court Road, and crossed the road to an Italian café.

He picked up a newspaper at the counter. Convoy losses in the Atlantic were continuing as was the bombing of British cities and

Rommel's offensive in North Africa. He couldn't imagine the States remaining neutral for ever. He was then interrupted by an elderly woman with a rather snooty accent informing him that as there was a notice on the café's paper stand stating that customers should pay for newspapers he should do so. He hadn't seen it and offered her the paper to return, reminding her that the 'Nero' in the café's name was pronounced with a short 'e,' not a long one. She replied with a condescending, 'Oh, touché,' and went out. He felt a little childlike; reminding himself to work on his hang-up about the British and their American ex-colony. He caught a bus to St. Paul's, feeling a sense of some wonderment, even a flash of fatalism at the cathedral still standing intact at the centre of the destruction surrounding it. Seeing 'Belgravia' on the front of another double-decker and liking the sound of the name, he jumped aboard it.

He enjoyed himself looking at the Georgian facades, Regency town houses and early Victorian buildings which, although sometimes tucked away in side streets, were invariably grand. After walking rather dreamily around Eaton Square he noticed, between two Edwardian mansions, a narrow bijou house with a flag of yellow, green and red horizontal stripes with a shield and spear towards one side almost half as large as the building it was hanging from. He turned down the street towards a public garden and, glancing again at the flag, saw a young African woman coming down the steps from the door beneath it and also moving in the direction of the garden.

He wasn't quite sure if it was her as most of her face was covered by a black headscarf. She suddenly stopped in the middle of the road as if sensing someone was watching her and turned towards him.

'What are you doing here? Are you following me?'

'No. I'm not.' He walked slowly towards her. 'I just happened to be... Is that your Embassy? Your father's?'

'Yes, why are you here?'

He explained.

'It was good of you to see them. But, I wonder why we're both here at this time in this street.'

'Of all the Embassies in all the world?'

'Are you coming to church with me?'

'A church?'

'Yes. The evening service, you know you'll like the building.'

'Okay, if it's not a long programme.'

CHAPTER SIX

'My father will be there; I'll introduce you as my teacher.' The smile was teasing.

'You think it's strange, too, don't you.'

'What is?'

'Meeting you. The last time I saw you -'

'You walked out.'

They moved on silently for a while until she said, 'Have you thought of what I said about -'

'I've tried not to.'

'Not facing it?'

'Denial's under rated.'

'You're being flippant.'

'A defence.'

'I've felt a little guilty about it, but I'm not taking it back.' She looked directly at him. 'Do you still want to come to church with me?' She asked it as if it represented a more significant request.

He walked beside her through a wide alley to a small square, one side of which was occupied by the church. He tried to concentrate on its architecture, a task made difficult by her presence and the way she kept turning her head to him, the headscarf delineating the shape of her cheekbones, enlarging her eyes. He looked around, almost formalising his observations: Victorian decorated gothic style, rag stone exterior, a French quality about the upper lattice of the windows and, as they went inside, painted columns supporting curved, pointed arches. It had an intimate feel and smelt like a church should. As a child he'd attended one at home that smelt exactly the same and had thought it was the cleaners using a detergent called, 'church smell soap.'

There was almost a full congregation, with five African men in the front row of the pews; the one in the centre, a large, broad-shouldered, slightly greying man he assumed was her father. There were two unoccupied seats together on the back row which they took as the service began.

It wasn't that dissimilar to the services of his youth, though less ritualistic and somehow more informal, the priest or vicar - he wasn't sure which - seemed more relaxed than those he remembered and sermonised quietly as if among friends or at least people he knew well. There was no choir, and a small organ, played quietly and without pomp, signalled the end of the service. As he stood and her father finished talking to the organist and walked towards them, she stepped into the aisle and said, 'Daddy, this is my teacher at university. He was looking around the area and we bumped into each other.'

Accompanied by a large, gold toothed grin his hand was gripped hard.

'Welcome. Do you attend church regularly?'

'No, afraid not, Mister Mnedi, I guess I'm an atheist.'

He looked at Robert and frowned. 'Atheism is like living in a dark cellar searching for a black cat that isn't there'.

'Guess we have that in common, uh? The difference is you've found it.' He saw her stifle a smile.

'Excuse me, there's someone I wish to talk to,' her father said and moved away to a group of men standing just in front of the entrance.

'Where are you staying tonight?' she asked.

'Not far away.'

'I'll come back with you if you like.' Her eyes had that slightly challenging, amused look he was getting pleasantly used to.

Then a siren began its scream. He'd never heard this sound before, it was ominous; it rose and fell with certainty, a kind of absolute. Her father looked through the lobby to her. 'Shelter,' he said, and strode towards a side exit of the churchyard.

'Come,' she said. They followed him to a large black car which they clambered into, sitting in the back, with one of the African men from the church driving them away. Robert asked her where they were going.

'To an Underground station, it's safer. My father asked the Ambassador if the Embassy could have its own shelter, but it wasn't possible.'

'So now you're with the hoi polloi?'

She frowned. 'Is that sarcasm?'

'Not really, sorry if you thought it was.'

'You're getting nervous aren't you. I haven't got used to this yet either; my father has, as well as a few million others.'

They stopped opposite Sloane Square station and joined people running down the escalator and stairs, except those with babies or small children who were merely hurrying. There was no panic; it seemed obvious that they were used to it. On the platform, people were laying bedding with some taking what looked like packed lunches and thermos flasks out of suit cases or paper bags and the occasional brief case.

CHAPTER SIX

More people came down, a few of them attempting to find space and make themselves comfortable by lying under the lines, seemingly taking it for granted that the electricity had been switched off immediately the siren went or perhaps sooner. The clothes most of them wore, the quality of the cases and the accents signalled different social strata than that of the East End he'd first seen and heard eighteen months previously. The platform soon became crowded though few people were standing, most sitting or lying down trying to get comfortable. There was a chocolate bar dispenser towards one end that two lads were trying to force open until a woman shouted at them, but as there was nowhere for them to run to they stood there a little stiffly and shamefaced. A rat ran along a line and fell, scrabbling, onto the face of a man underneath. An arm brushed it away, the man perhaps trying to sleep, though it wasn't that late. Somebody began playing an accordion and a few people started singing, while a young man and a woman jumped down from the other end of the platform and disappeared into the tunnel. He wondered how far into it they would go in giving the sexually analogous train entering a tunnel image the bizarre twist they were, maybe, intending.

Her father was standing against the tiled wall next to the circular station sign, two of the Africans at the side of him. He was looking around him as if to organise something, to oversee the giving of aid, of nutrients. Prudence sat down near him, Robert sat next to her. There was relatively little noise; people were orderly, seemingly accepting it all. She leaned her head on his shoulder for a moment. He liked it; felt a warmth; a belonging.

There was a siren again; he wasn't sure where it came from but it could be heard clearly. This one, though, was deeper and steadier.

'It's the all-clear,' she said. 'Perhaps it was a false alarm and there'll be no raid tonight.'

It registered then that during her sporadic absences from college she could have been with her father, wondering if there would be another raid and they would have to come down here.

People busied themselves again, picking up bedding and bags, clearing away food wrappers, shutting cases and making their way towards the bottom of the escalators and stairs. Robert and Prudence joined them. Only one escalator was moving so they climbed the stairs, went through the booking hall, out of the station and on to the pavement again. Her father was standing in the middle of it waiting for them. He held out his hand as they approached and shook Robert's again.

'I need to go now, my daughter tells me you are teaching her well, which is good; continue to do so.' He smiled at her. 'I shall see you later.' and, followed by the Africans, went back to the car and was driven off.

After watching her father leave, she again asked where Robert was staying. 'I shouldn't think the trains will be running yet, but there are buses.'

'Are you going to walk to the stop with me?'

She didn't answer, just continued walking at his side.

'You have an intellectualized disbelief in faith, don't you. Why? Frightened to believe?'

He'd never considered it before; it seemed ridiculous; it surely was a great leap of trust to fully believe in a superhuman deity, to place...

'You're analysing that now, aren't you.'

'It's a good question.'

They arrived at the stop. There was quite a queue; somebody had once told him that the queue had been invented by the British. He could believe it. They boarded a bus that was going to Holborn and sat silently on the top deck looking out at more sandbagged buildings and a large row of shops that were partly demolished. It was getting dark now; there were no streetlights. The bus carried on for a little while then stopped, the conductor shouting up the stairs that it terminated here. They got off and made their way towards the hotel.

'You liked the last question I asked you, so what about this one. Do you want me to stay with you tonight or do I walk away from *you* this time?'

He purposely didn't answer. They walked on.

The building was dirty, paint peeling from its sashes and entrance door, its concrete steps crumbling. The woman leaning on a wooden counter a few yards down the hallway looked up from stroking a puppy.

'Evening, Mister Costain.' She looked at Prudence. 'Yes, Miss, what can I do for you?'

She held out a passport. 'My embassy,' she said in an English accent that could have cut glass, 'is unavailable this evening, but I may return later.' As her visa was being examined, she leant her head briefly against his. 'Give her some money,' she whispered.

CHAPTER SIX

He did, holding out the first note he found in his wallet. The woman took it and as she turned to put it in a tin box behind her, he said in a low voice, 'Your name's on that passport.'

'And?'

'Don't you mind? This sort of thing's seen as immoral, well, it is in the States, hence the 'Mr. and Mrs. Smith' thing.'

'I think we're worth more than 'Smith,' don't you?'

The woman handed back the passport and took a key from a bunch beside her. She raised an eyebrow. 'The same room Mister Costain, or a different one?'

'I'm sure it will do very well,' said Prudence in her new accent. He took the key.

'It's at the top of the first flight, the room facing.'

He looked at Prudence; she was already climbing the stairs.

He opened a shabby, dark green door, a similar colour to the London railway bridges he'd noticed, and she followed him in. He looked around at greying net curtains, a mahogany wardrobe, a deep red shade around a bulb hanging from a cracked ceiling under which a purple rose pattern embossed the wallpaper, and a threadbare rug covering some of the floorboards next to a rather narrow double bed. Using her upper crust accent and looking at him with exaggerated archness, she said, 'Does the room really matter?' Surely we have our own delicious dalliances to enjoy whatever the surroundings.'

He laughed, the tension melting from him. 'You do that accent so well. Where did you get it from?'

She sat on the edge of the bed. 'If you had been to as many diplomatic functions as I have, you, too, could learn it.'

He looked down at her and kissed her gently on the mouth.

She looked up. 'What's that for?'

'For being you, I guess.'

'It's okay you know, you're allowed to transfer the stereotype to reality; you may treat me as an object of sex.'

There had only been one girl before Jess. Was he trying to make up for it, be like the big boys? He asked her why, if she'd wanted to seduce him on her birthday, she hadn't made it more obvious.

'How?'

'Wearing different clothes maybe.'

'Cleavage? Glitz? That sort of thing?' She shook her head and started to speak in Bantu; making clicking sounds before her consonants. He had no idea what she was saying. He asked her to stop.

'Why, does it make me more African? More alien?'

He stopped her talking. She was right, the room wasn't there anymore. And there was no raid that night.

She was so pleased when Mister Costain said he would come to see them and tell them how Keith was getting on. It was such a nice letter, too. Fred hadn't said much at all; she supposed that with him it was a case of if not hearing anything to the contrary he was alright. He didn't seem to like Americans, 'Bleedin' Yanks,' he'd sometimes call them, she didn't know why. He was often saying that everything they had was bigger over there; the cars, the steaks - chance would be a fine thing - the buildings, the land, and everybody had more money than we did and they shouted a lot, too. He tried to imitate their accents sometimes, it was a sort of growly sound with lots of 'R's' in and he sneered when he did it. He didn't like their films or what they called 'movies' much anyway, he didn't really go to the pictures, not even to pop in to see his sisters at the Broadway. He thought Americans were showing off; she supposed he was jealous of them. He was jealous of Keith as well, according to Gwen. She told her a few years ago that he was a possessive man and didn't like her giving Keith her love. Perhaps that was why he didn't seem to miss him like she did; well, he rarely mentioned him.

But it didn't make sense. When Keith was a baby Fred would come in from work and, if she was in the hall, push by her and say, 'Where's Keith, is he in bed?' 'He'd be halfway up the stairs before she could say yes. He seemed to like talking to him and kissing him, but then it stopped, and he never read to him, he'd just say, 'Goodnight, son.' and he fussed if he thought he was dallying over his supper and told him to hurry up and that he should be in bed, as if he wanted him out of the way so he could be with just her. It wasn't as if they did anything though, they just listened to the wireless or she would read, he never did, unless it was the 'Mirror.' If she was listening to a singer she liked, especially an American one, he'd say something like, 'What d'yer want to listen to 'im for, you can't understand what he's singin' about.' And he didn't like it when she spent time upstairs with Flo when they did each other's hair, particularly when Harry was home; perhaps he felt left out even more then. He'd probably feel better if he had friends to go out with

CHAPTER SIX

sometimes other than Albert and Harry, but they were family and didn't count. He was quite shy really, didn't think he had much to offer. He didn't offer *her* much. She sensed it from the beginning, but she liked him, she was still fond of him she supposed. Gwen couldn't have been right, surely; however insecure he was how could any man feel like that about his own son? He was jealous in some ways, though. If she talked to a man in, say, a shop or somewhere - not that he went shopping with her much - he seemed to get a bit restless as if he didn't like her paying attention to other people. That was it; he wanted the attention, and perhaps it was due to the way his father had treated him. She felt suddenly depressed. She didn't seem to see as much of Flo lately and was missing Keith.

She thought Mr. Costain seemed a nice man immediately she saw him, he was tall and smooth skinned and you could see he'd recently shaved, she liked that in a man; he wasn't much younger than her. Fred seemed reluctant to get up off his chair and he'd left her to open the front door. He was so easy to speak to as well, though maybe she shouldn't have told him so much about Fred; she didn't talk to many people about those things.

The delight that had obliterated his guilt had begun to leave him by the time his train eased into Norwich Thorpe station. He'd woken late, holding her close to him; the dark shape that had slipped under the sheets after she'd undressed was now still, breathing evenly, her skin, to him, so smooth as to be without pores and her hair, still short and boyish, added to her in a way he couldn't quite describe. He forced himself to move away from her and dress. There was no need to rush, but if he didn't leave now he felt he never would. As she woke he kissed her on the forehead and told her he'd see her soon.

'That was rather platonic wasn't it?' she asked, slowly sitting up.

'No, I need to go, I'm afraid. I'd like to keep here for ever, Prudence.'

'That's probably only the second time you've used my name.'

He closed the door quietly behind him and, ignoring the 'Sleep well, Mr. Costain?' from the woman in the hall, left.

On the train back he felt a little like an alien from another world who had done something enormously wrong in leaving it to come to this one and had to return as soon as he could before somebody discovered that he'd left. Billy came into his mind; Christ, what would he say about this.

Jess was in the long room when he came in. 'How did it go? Did you look around?'

He told her where he'd been. 'Belgravia was the most interesting, including a church I actually went in. I saw the African student coming out of her Embassy. Her father -'

'Why do you call her that?'

Why did he mention her? to seem ingenuous, honest, innocent? Or was there something in him that wanted to be interrogated, found out; forgiven? He asked what she'd been doing. Half of her time she'd spent with Keith.

'He was quiet, I think he missed you. His mother rang to speak with him for a little while; she was pleased you'd gone to see her. Did you meet his dad?'

'For a little while, yes. He had a pretty tough time as a kid it would seem; could be a case of damage creating damage, but it's too late for him and he's coping with it anyway. He's probably a deferential victim of a class system in which he's at the base of the pyramid looking up at the hierarchical strata above. He probably eagerly embraces the very system that exploits him.'

'Tell it to Norman.'

'Where's Keith now?'

'In his room, I think.'

They heard footsteps hurrying down the stairs and he came into the room. 'Hello, Mister Robert, did you see my mum?'

'Yes, and your dad, they send their love and I've told 'em you're okay, but I didn't see your brother, he was asleep.'

'Were there any bombs?'

'Not as far as I know, though there were sirens for a short while so we went into a Tube station and sat on the platform with lots of other people.'

'Who's 'we'?' Jess interrupted.

'Cor, I'd like to have done that. Did you go to Plaistow station?'

'Yep, I walked past your school where the Headmaster looks down out of his window when you're in assembly.'

'And where Mister Baxter the maths teacher said I'd land up being a dustman because I wasn't good at formulas and I told him they didn't tell us about whether things were real or not, only numbers and measurements, which are just more numbers'

'You're quite right, and forget the garbage collector stuff. Betcha liked the English teacher, uh?'

CHAPTER SIX

'Yes, but we had a new one and he thought I copied my composition from a book, but I didn't, *I* wrote it.'

Robert felt this was probably one amongst many wounds in his non-acknowledgement; he'd been blocked off, he couldn't share his mind; perhaps his father was frightened he wouldn't be able to eventually understand what his son thought, the way he thought.

He discussed this a little later when he and Norman were alone.

'You're probably right on both counts, but, of course, he'll have to go back eventually, probably sooner rather than later, they can't keep raiding us for ever, can they?'

'Who knows, but he's our problem now. His mother's a caring one, but I can't see her ever getting close to him, there's anxiety there, too. However, it's work again tomorrow.' He asked how Prudence was progressing with him.

'Mnedi? She's perceptive isn't she; she's making up for lost time well; strong on critique.'

They discussed a few more students then called it a night. In their room Jess was asleep on the far edge of the bed.

She didn't turn up at his lectures or seminar the next day or the day after. In between them he thought of her in church, watching her kneel with bowed head, completely still. It wasn't a precious place, no Catholic gold and glitz, just some dulled oak, acanthus leaf capitals, plain painted walls. A sparrow would have looked down on black coats, some grey heads, a corner painting and tomb and maybe hear a violin dirge in a nave that had housed hatreds and saccharin cant and probably never seen a floral 'Grandpa;' and there would be the spirit's weakening to the body, the fidgets, coughs, the desire for the wine and smoked eels, the toilet... He was aware that he was visualising the place again in order not to prolong the image of her at prayer.

He pictured her afterwards in the Underground station, sitting impassively between him and her standing father, once or twice rising to help a woman with a child then relaxing again when someone else did or the woman coped herself. People had been good humoured, only the occasional raucous laugh, a drunk or screaming baby; and he could still feel her cheek on his shoulder.

He purposely and unnecessarily worked late into the night phrasing test questions, marking the few pieces of work he had left to mark and drafting lectures on topics he was familiar with anyway.

KEEFIE

Jess never commented, she was always asleep when he got to bed, whenever it was.

CHAPTER 7

There were two further essays from her in his pigeon hole. He had a quick look to see if there was anything else, there wasn't. She was clearing her backlog and was almost up to date with him. As usual, they were well argued and direct; in one, deftly destroying a theory of economic growth in Africa by a minor American sociologist and providing insights in another that he thought even Marx may have overlooked. Perhaps this is what she'd been doing instead of attending seminars. On his way home, looking out of the bus window at more hedges, more fields, more barns, he made up his mind to go to her flat the next afternoon.

During a silent evening meal, Norman not joining them as he'd gone to London to stay with an old colleague for the weekend, Jess broke the silence as she got up to wash the dishes. She began casually.

'I was talking to someone from the Principal's office at lunch and she started talking about one of your students.' He was finishing his meal and nodded absently.

'It was a girl who, apparently, told something to the Principal's secretary who's supposed to be her friend who then mentioned it to someone else, and so on.'

He wiped his mouth with a napkin. 'Mentioned what?'

'That she'd had a fling with a guy.'

He felt a prick of fear and forced a disinterested, 'It happens.'

'Yeh, it does, and it happened in London with a lecturer from this place, good old London University Anglia.'

Her voice started to rise. 'And you should know, Rob, uh? And what a name; Prudence. What's it about, some sort of social class study; the poor but dishonest carpenter from the Bronx and the diplomat's daughter? Pleased with yourself?' She began to shout. 'A Zulu, eh? What *is* it about black pussy, where does it all come from, teenage flicks of tits bouncing in tribal dances? Or is it really about showing your colleagues you're as liberal as the next man?'

She took a step into the room, a plate in her hand. 'How will you feel when two old ladies in a café serve her burnt toast and a dirty mug because they know she's with you, eh? And how long d'you think it'll last?'

She turned and hurled the plate on the kitchen floor, its sound filling the room, pieces of it scattering across the rug at his feet. He tried to think logically, she surely wouldn't have named him, would she? It wasn't... He stood.

'Jess, stop. It's -'

'It's what, a mirage? Something - what d'you call it - not amenable to sense data? Perhaps it didn't happen, eh?'

'No, it's just -'

'Just *what?*'

He couldn't seem to speak properly. 'I'm sorry, it was... I've never done this before, ever.'

Her eyes widened in mock surprise. 'And you won't again? There's a good boy.'

He tried to think. 'It shouldn't have happened, but... I just needed to share, I was - '

'What, your wonderful intellect? You need it recognised, is that it? All the theories, all the architecture. What about what *I* want to share?'

'But we have, we do, don't we?'

'You're not so articulate now are you, the words all gone have they?'

Her voice rose higher. 'You've got the other lecturers, the students, Norman; she's more attractive than those though, isn't she? Can't have rock and roll with Norman, can you. You can't compartmentalise, you want it all in one person, it all has to go into one doesn't it; looks, intelligence, interests, and what about humour? Have lots of laughs do you?' Has she got it all, then? You're a child.'

He looked away from her. He felt his vocabulary had been stolen.

'I've suspected this since I saw you with her at that office party. Then you just happened to run into her when - '

'I *did* just happen to.'

'I've heard about her from the admin. people; how clever she is, the style she's got and she's rich, too, that's what they say, born to a family with money. And there's Keith, he loves being with you and you use him as some sort of research project. You say you went to see his parents to reassure them about their son, but you really went to see what bad influences could have affected him, didn't you. Yes? He looks up to you and you say you're getting close to him, but you're using him. You're such a hypocrite.'

'It's not like that with him and it won't happen again with her.'

CHAPTER SEVEN

'It doesn't matter; I won't be here to care. You can have your transatlantic adventure, your intellectual journeys, your... fucking a black woman.'

She almost screamed the last words. She was silent for a few seconds then pushed past him and ran upstairs.

He sat down again at the table and looked around him; walls, ceiling, fireplace, window, just objects that were hard and inimical, that couldn't help him. He stood to go up the stairs after her, but felt it pointless. He knew he was panicking, but not what would stop it. Prudence; he needed to see her. Norman had left him the car; Robert had driven him to the station and would pick him up on Sunday evening. He went out to it, trying to remember how he'd gotten to her flat. He tried to drive slowly, darkening country lanes weren't the places to speed on. He drove along Prince Of Wales Road trying to recognise her block. He turned into the street and stopped outside the house; there were no lights on in any of the rooms. He rang her bell several times then knocked; there was no one in the ground floor flat either. He stood on the doorstep replaying the scene in the farmhouse. He felt a corrosive guilt beginning; felt pitiable, but not deserving of pity.

He went back, this house, too, was completely dark. Their room couldn't be seen from the drive, but he expected it to be lit. It wasn't. He went in and up the stairs, knocked on their door without response then tried Norman's. It was locked. How had she left so quickly? The buses weren't that regular, perhaps she'd called a taxi, but where would she go? Downstairs, he cleared the fractured pieces of china from the carpet and lay on the sofa. He didn't want to lie alone in their bed. There were slices of light appearing at the curtain's edges before he finally slept.

When he woke, he saw though the open door Keith sitting at the table eating a chunk of bread.

'Hello, Mister Robert, you were asleep in the long room.'

'Yeh, I've got a cough, didn't want to disturb Jess.'

'I'm going to play with Jamie when he's finished with the cows.'

'Sure, I'll be around.'

He cooked some food for both of them and by the time he'd finished, Keith had gone across to the shippen. He tried to eat something, but his throat was too tight. He rang the university and got through to Personnel. He mumbled his name and gave

Prudence's. 'I need to find out why she hasn't been attending seminars; it would be useful if I could have her telephone number.'

He was given it and went into the hall and used it. It kept ringing.

Keith appeared. 'Jamie said I could stay with him and his uncle till tea time.'

'Fine, enjoy yourself.' The boy ran off.

He went to their room. It looked just the same; neat and tidy. He couldn't bring himself to look in the wardrobe. He tried the number again. It was answered.

'It's me,' he said.

'Why haven't you contacted me before?'

'I didn't know where you were. I went to your flat earlier, you weren't there.'

'I was in the campus library as usual; I have work to do, remember?'

'I need to see you.'

'The feeling's mutual.'

'No, it's important. We have to talk.'

'Is that all?'

'Can you meet me?'

'Where?'

'Best it's private. There's a lane at the back of the farm, Mellands Lane. You get to it off the Ripton Road, the name of the farm's on a sign at the back, it's not a big sign, but you'll find it.' He asked her if she could make it in an hour. She hoped there was nothing wrong.

He'd have preferred to be in the shippen feeling a warmth and comfort from its recently vacated cows. He would have looked at the steaming pats of faeces, the wooden rails holding the animals in, the full churns and empty buckets and thought of absurd opposites like Broadway, Park Avenue and the Rockefeller Museum. He was a long way from home. He thought of the phrase, 'He girded his loins,' left the house and tramped his way the quarter of a mile across the back field to the lane.

He leant on the wooden gate feeling the situation had a kind of surreal theatricality as he looked up the road for her car. It came soon, pulling over in front of him. She was wearing the headscarf again and as she got out he saw a long brown dress with red and blue abstract shapes that almost covered her feet.

'It's modern traditional Zulu,' she said, standing in front of the car. 'Scared I'm going to frighten the horses?'

CHAPTER SEVEN

'Why d'you keep -'

'Being flippant? Why do you think?' Are you going to open that gate instead of hiding behind it?'

He unlatched it and swung it away from her.

'It's a built-in sarcasm to ward off the world and perhaps you're the part of the world I have to protect myself from. You're going to tell me you don't want to see me any more, aren't you; well, outside of the classroom.'

'I do want to see you, but -'

''He wanted to layeth with her.''

'I can't see you again.'

'Frightened of your wife?'

'She found out, you told someone.'

'I shouldn't have.' She was silent. 'But, maybe it's a blessing in disguise, and don't tell me off for using a religious cliché. I assume she hasn't forgiven you; do you want her to, Robert? Is she going to leave you? Is that painful? It's only the two of you, anyway, there are no children are there.'

He didn't know what to say. Then, 'I'm going to teach you and mark your work, and that's it.' He went back through the gate then turned towards her. 'I was going to say sorry, but after that, no.'

He strode off the way he'd come, across the middle of the field, feeling angry and, the faster he moved, the more alone.

He didn't want to play with Jamie any more, he was always talking about country things like pigs and milking and tractors and although he had all these trees to climb, he never did. He didn't like football much and when he did play he kicked the ball a long way, but never went to get it and bring it back. He was okay in the goal they made between two milk churns, though. He talked funny, too, ''ave yew gotta big 'owse in London, bor?' he'd say, or 'There's a gerl wot lives at Peter Bovey's farm that's gotta big pair o' tits, she's boo'ful.' He was someone to play with, but he didn't really like him, though Mister Robert thought he did. He liked his uncle a bit, but not when, the other morning, he shouted at him because he'd tripped over one of his rabbit snares that were hidden around the fields. He swore at him and cursed him, something about God striking him. His mother would have called it blasphemy.

He didn't know where Jamie was so started walking around the edge of the farm in the dried-up stream where the mauve flowers grew. He walked up to where the stream had gone under the ground by the gate and then began again on the other side. He was about to climb out of it when he saw Mister Robert at the gate with his wellies on, he looked like a proper farmer. He wore jeans which he did in the house sometimes as if he was a cowboy, but he wasn't Gene Autry or Roy Rogers who wore a little scarf and was always smiling.

He'd never seen the lady who was with him before. She was black. He'd seen pictures of black people in the photos his dad showed him when he was in India, but she was different; she was really dark and tall and had black eyes. Mum would have liked her eyes, they were big. She'd have liked her; she'd have said, 'Pleased to meet you, I'm sure.' and given her a cup of tea. Dad called black people 'darkies' or 'wogs.' He'd heard uncle Albert say they were 'nig nogs.' But, he didn't like her, he felt frightened; she looked angry and her hair was sort of sticking up. He wondered if it was the lady Jess had shouted at Mister Robert about last night which had woken him up. He'd heard her say her name when he had come back from seeing mum, it began with a 'P,' but he couldn't remember it. They hadn't seen him so he hid behind a tree.

The lady was shouting a bit, then Mister Robert did, too, shaking his head, then he turned around and started walking back across the field, leaving the gate open. He saw the lady get into a car and slam the door then she got out of it again and went over to the gate and stood in the gap in the trees where she shouted again. She scared him more when she shouted and he didn't like to think of her upsetting Mister Robert. Perhaps he was scared of her as well and she'd upset Jess. He liked Jess 'cos she looked after him. He moved away from behind the tree and ran over to her and pushed her. He pushed her hard and she slipped and fell. Her head hit the root of a tree, he heard the noise. She just lay there; she didn't do anything, nothing. He didn't mean to hurt her.

He knew she needed help and started running after Robert, but if he told him what he'd done, he would tell his mum. He stopped and ran back again. He looked down at her. Her eyes were closed and there was some blood on the side of her face. He took a handkerchief out of his pocket which mum had ironed before he came here and which he hadn't used. He unfolded it and placed it on the blood. He then ran out of the field and along the lane away from the car.

CHAPTER SEVEN

Robert got back to the house and without taking his boots off went upstairs; he needed to see Jess. He went to their room and opened the wardrobe doors; her clothes had gone. As he pulled out the drawer at its base he saw that she'd taken her underwear also. Most of the ornaments had gone from the dresser. He imagined her sweeping a hand across the top of it, the objects dropping into a hastily grabbed bag. There were two Lladro figurines left, a girl with a cake teasing a dog and two children in a nursery fight, one holding a pillow above her head like a murderous leg of lamb; he tried not to see himself as the small, blue-coated boy curled up with a protective arm above his head. He sat on their bed, the house seemed very empty. The phone downstairs rang. It was her.

'I'm just letting you know I'm okay, I'm staying with someone from work. Don't try to find me, leave things as they are.'

The line went dead. He went up to the room again as if she was still there, as if he would find solace.

He went out into the yard then around the back of the house to the orchard, noticing the apples had started to grow, Worcesters, his favourites, despite Norman laughing at his pronunciation of their name. He went around to the front, walked across the lawn and pointlessly wiped his boots on the iron scraper by the side of the doorstep then walked down the drive to the entrance. He looked towards the village then went back and poured himself a drink.

As he went to their room, having made up his mind that he wasn't going to sleep anywhere else, he'd just have to face lying there without her, the phone rang again. It was the foreman, Doug. An hour before, a man had knocked on his door asking for the use of his phone, it was an emergency. He'd been driving along Mellands Lane when he stopped to look at the view across the fields, thinking, as he saw another car there, that someone else had had the same thought. He'd seen a woman lying under a tree a few yards from him with blood on her face and moaning in pain. She was African, apparently. He'd noticed Doug's cottage moments before as he drove past it. He hadn't touched her except to put his jacket over her and get a cushion from his car for her head, not doing any more in case she'd broken something and he did further damage. He'd rung Emergency and driven back to the gate to wait for the ambulance.

'twere lucky 'e found 'er, she could 'ave laid there fer 'ours, though she could well 'ave been for all we know. Thought I'd tell yer 'cos 'twere on the farm's land. Reckon she'll be in the Norwich General be now.'

What had happened? He imagined her looking at his receding back and in a fit of pique kicking the nearest solid object, the gate or a tree and hurting her foot and then falling. What a frustrating, unhappy moment. He couldn't picture anyone attacking her; why would they, except that she was different. 'Different' could be perceived as a threat, creating an instant dislike, a fearful response. But there had been nobody near and no vehicle had passed while he was with her. He thanked the foreman and phoned the hospital. It took a while for anyone to ascertain who had been brought in and why. Eventually he was told that she'd hit her head, was concussed and had a hair line fracture above an ankle. He asked if he could see her. He couldn't, she was still being treated. Would she want to see him, anyway? He went to the kitchen to make a coffee, looking eastward out of its window at the dusk coming from over the hill. He wondered where Keith was.

He was running really fast, like when they had races at school in the playground and when he played football, though the others nearly always caught him up; he was tricky with a ball and could dribble well, but was knocked over pretty easily. Once, a big boy who was in a team they were playing against on the cinder pitch at Becton Road, smashed into Terry Bowhay so Keith ran at him and barged him over, but afterwards he felt like someone in the cartoons when they got hurt and stars spun round their head. He probably ran like that the day before he came to the farm when he scooted out of Jock the barber's at the end of Church Alley because he got his razor out and it scared him. Dad made him go back again.

He stopped when he got to the crossroads and wondered what he should do. He saw a bus slowing down at a bus stop and ran to it and jumped on. It was a yellow one and he couldn't go upstairs like he did at home 'cos it didn't have one, and there was no conductor to give his money to. He sat at the back, not sure whether he'd got on because it would take him away from the farm or because it said 'Norwich Thorpe Stn.' on the front and he'd seen the outside of the station when he'd turned round to look at it when Norman had first driven him to the farm. There wasn't much traffic; there were probably more tractors and ploughs in the fields than cars on the roads. There were only two other people on the bus, one of them had

CHAPTER SEVEN

a dog that kept yapping. When he went over the park with mum sometimes and a dog, pulling on a lead, barked at him, its owner would say, 'It's alright missus, it won't hurt him,' and mum used to say a little while afterwards, 'How are we supposed to bloody know?' They passed a stile between some hedges and he thought of the lady lying on the ground, but pretended she wasn't hurt, just lying there for a little while and getting up again.

It seemed a long way to Norwich. The lane got wider and there were more houses and buildings and more traffic. He saw the spire of a big church he supposed was the cathedral; it was a lot higher than West Ham church which didn't have a spire, it had a turret like the sides of the farmhouse. When they stopped he got off last and the driver looked at him in a funny way, but didn't ask for any money.

The station wasn't as big as some of those in London, there wasn't so much noise and there was only one train in. There was a little buffet at the beginning of one of the platforms and instead of buying sweets he asked for a cup of tea. He'd never bought one before and felt grown up, but not properly because he had to look up at the man behind the counter and reach a bit to give him the money. As he stood there waiting the man told him to take a seat and he'd bring it over. He sat in a corner and when it came, put sugar and milk in, feeling like an adult, though to be a proper one he'd have to roll a cigarette and smoke it like dad. There was a glass ashtray on the table with 'Capstan' on the side; he knew it was something to do with ships and wondered why it was on an ashtray. A man came in with a newspaper and sat near him, it was 'The Times,' he'd never read a copy of that before. '60th Raid On London.' the headline said. He was glad mum and Lenny had a shelter to go down.

He looked out of the window at the train. There wasn't a driver or a fireman in the engine cab and there were no people in the carriages yet. He thought of it starting and wrote 'pulsating pistons' and 'a steam hiss of motion' on his notepad which aunt Gwen had told him he should always have with him in case he wanted to write things down or draw something. He went out, walked along the platform where the train was, opened a carriage door and sat next to it looking out the opposite window. He could see a porter on the next platform and drew him pushing the luggage bent over like a scarecrow wearing a cap. He sketched a signal box and some trees he could see past the far end of another platform then tried to draw the black lady's face. He shaded it with criss-cross lines and drew a smile on it; her teeth seemed very white so he tried to draw some blood on them, but didn't have a red pencil. He tore it from his pad then thought he'd draw his mother, but though he got her nose right because it was long he couldn't do the eyes, he wasn't very good at eyes. He tried to capture the lady's face again and drew thick, curved lips and big eyes which he made as black as he could without putting his pencil through the paper, but he knew she didn't look like that. She wasn't pretty like, say, Iris Miller, more... attractive; mum thought aunt Rose was attractive. He thought of the farm and tried to draw a cow, but it looked more like a camel, so he did a sheep's face. He put a few bushes behind it and, as it was looking down, put the lady's face under it as if the sheep was kissing her or eating her. He remembered her name now, it was Prudence.

He looked at the drawing again. He rubbed away some of the black of the eye with the rubber tip of his pencil to make a glint and made the nose a little smaller. It was actually like her now; he could see her clearly. She was different from everybody, but was nice, really. She'd been wearing a dress with bright colours when he'd pushed her, her hip had pressed in a little bit; he'd have liked to have touched her bottom. He made her hair darker and more sticking up and turned the curve of her lips up at the corners so she was sort of smiling. He wondered why Jess didn't seem to like her, why she shouted about her to Robert. He thought of Joyce, mum's friend, who used to pick him up and pretend to shake him when he was little and who was supposed to marry cousin Gordon, but, according to mum, had run off with a bandleader. Was Robert going to do something like that with Prudence then? She might still be lying there, he wasn't sure anyone could see her from the lane.

The lights were coming on above the platform; it was getting chilly. He stepped down from the carriage, walked along the platform towards the buffet place and sat inside again. He wanted to see mum and aunt Gwen. He got up and ran back along the side of the train, dropping and picking up his drawing on the way, and looked at the front of the engine to see if 'London' or 'Liverpool Street' was written on it; he could find his way home from there. It wasn't. The porter he'd drawn was pushing luggage on this platform now and stopped and asked what he was doing.

'Does this train go to London, please?'

'It do, but not fer an 'our. Where's yer mum and dad then?'

CHAPTER SEVEN

He didn't know what to say. He ran back past the buffet to the station entrance and stopped. He saw a bus shelter, went inside and read the time table; the Ripton bus was due in five minutes. It was on time. It was almost dark now.

Robert rang Doug several times before he answered; he'd been with his nephew assisting a sheep to give birth to twins. He wanted to know if Jamie was there. He was, but didn't know where Keith was, he hadn't seen him since the day before when his offer to teach him to milk a cow had been turned down and they'd played odds and ends against the shippen wall for while. He was asked where the places were they liked playing in.

'Well, he played more 'n me 'cos I do things on the farm fer me uncle, but we used to have runnin' races sometimes till he wandered off somewhere or went back to his school work with you or your wife or be on his own. He used to like sittin' in the barn sometimes and drawin'.'

Robert thanked him and went to the barn, though he couldn't visualize him there; it was large and at night its perspective seemed exaggerated, giving it an almost aggressively monolithic look. He switched the lights on. There was enough hay to hide a school load of boys. He shouted Keith's name; it echoed away without response. He saw a square of paper on the floor at the side of the door. It was a sketch of a baby or infant, he wasn't sure where the arbitrary distinction lay. He guessed it was supposed to be Lenny; he had a fist in the air as if he was punching something.

He went back to the house and up to the boy's room and knocked in case he'd returned. He looked around it, it probably wasn't a typical child's room, nothing pinned on the walls, no drawings, posters or photos, but then this was his temporary home, though he couldn't imagine him having anything on the walls of his room in his permanent one either. There was a new exercise book that Jess had bought him lying on a chair. There were a few rhyming poems and some attempts at alliteration: 'cluttered curving cambered coast' was one such, 'sifting sprawling sepia sand' another. A coat was hanging inside the door, a jumper, shirt, underwear and a pair of worsted shorts crammed in the bedside chest. Robert looked at his watch and thought for a while. The last bus to Ripton from anywhere had gone.

He was the only person in the shelter. He pulled his jacket collar up wishing he'd put his jumper on, mum would have made him, she was always fussing: blacken his shoes, tie the laces tightly or he'd trip over, put his cap on properly; do his buttons up. Now, he didn't have to do anything, but wished she was here to tell him what to do. People seemed to like her; he heard Frankie's mum say to Mrs. Miller once that she had 'principles.' He had a secret; he knew that if anyone in the turning died somebody would knock for mum to go to the house and close the dead person's eyes, but she'd never told him so didn't know that he knew. Dad said that people put pennies on corpses' eyes so they wouldn't come open. And if someone had a baby at home, Teapot Lil would go over to help; a sort of unofficial midwife. He used to think that what with Wendy and Alfie's dad knowing about business, Mrs. Foxcroft's daughter being a typist and Mr. Miller being a coach driver, all the people in the street could be driven to a bank in London and be given forms to fill out for lots of money.

When the bus came, it stopped with the driver exactly level with the bus stop, sitting still, looking at him.

'You a'comin' then? Where yer goin'?'

He didn't answer. There was an old lady sitting at the back of the bus who was also looking at him.

'Well, goo'night young man,' said the driver and closed the door.

He got up from the bench and wanted to run to the door and bang on it so it would open again, but thought of the carriage he'd been sitting in and that if he waited in it for a little while he could go to London. The bus drove away, the old lady turning her head to stare at him through the back window. He turned and ran through the entrance again and nearly collided with the porter.

'It's you again, what you doin' 'ere, you playin' about or summat or thinkin' o' goin' back to that train? It's been cancelled, anyway, no more 'onight, bor, last one's gone.'

He walked away, looking back at the empty station: someone was putting old newspapers in a bin, a man with a spanner walked to a van, and the wooden shutters of the ticket office windows were being closed. He could hide in a corner till the first train in the morning, but it would be cold. He saw Prudence's face again, it was white and red like the pastry mum splashed jam on before baking; she'd be cold as well. He wanted to put his jacket on her to keep her shoulders warm. He wondered if his handkerchief was still on her face. He

CHAPTER SEVEN

looked up the road where the Ripton bus had gone. The porter was frowning at him.

'You alright? Yer know what yer doin' do yer?'

'Yes, thank you.'

He ran along the road towards the lights of the city centre.

CHAPTER 8

He was beginning to get anxious about Keith, it was late and he had no idea where the boy was, nor did Doug or Jamie. He pushed thoughts of Jess and Prudence away and walked around the house once more shouting his name just to make sure he wasn't in it. He went to the shippen, the orchard, even the barn again before returning to the room for a torch. Going out into the back field he bent under the low branches of a greening tree and stepped down into the dried stream where his light illuminated short grass, weeds and surprisingly established flowers. It could, he supposed, be seen as a kind of long, enchanted grove. Keith would have liked it; he wanted to find him and tell him about it, they could walk it together sometime.

He couldn't rid himself of thoughts of Jess and assumed she wasn't far away; in Dereham or Ripton, maybe. Perhaps she'd just take some time off from her job then return. He saw a badger in front of him; a few months ago he may not have recognised what it was, since being here he'd seen quite a few. Further on, a bat flitted by his ear. He thought of Nagel's question of what it was like to be a bat, pointing out that when we talk about conscious mental states like pain and visual experiences, we often run objective and subjective conceptions of these together, never bothering to specify whether it's the subjective experience or objective features of the psychological role and physical make-up we're alluding to. He stopped himself; he was beginning to recognize that, as well as a satisfying, though often short-lived excitement when proselytizing in a lecture theatre, he also tended to intellectualize when he couldn't face something painful, either memories or that which was happening at the time. Another one passed on his other side.

'I don't give a shit what it's like to be you, baby,' he shouted, feeling immediately childlike and stupid. He moved along faster, calling the boy's name again.

He felt restless, his hands wanting to do something. He hadn't worked with wood since he'd been over here; sure, there were bits and pieces he'd done at the farm: in the shippen, some fencing, a kitchen cupboard, taken some shavings off a door, but not creating anything interesting. Maybe he could make something for Norman,

CHAPTER EIGHT

he still felt he owed him, a period chair or desk perhaps, something he'd value; Keith could make a sketch of it. He'd made an Italian sideboard for Jess's parents who they'd lived with for a while when they first got married, but that was then, when he and Billy saw a lot of each other and had some good times: the Bowery Theater on lower East Side, the Jewish Theater on 2nd, Eddie Cantor, Katie Smith, Rose Marie; he remembered he and his friend stubbornly supporting vaudeville for years before movies closed it down. He'd written just one letter to him, the first week he'd arrived here. He walked on, the bed of the stream now turning at the corner of the field and running towards the gate. He hadn't thought of Jess or Prudence for at least ten minutes.

It was, he knew, probably useless looking for him here, but he was becoming a little addicted to the torchlight catching the branches and burgeoning leaves, a moth or two, and images of Jess's angry face and Prudence's scowling one appearing in front of him. What if the boy had decided to return home, he could have money saved, but that would be more an instinctual impetus than a decision, a panic perhaps, but from what cause? Maybe an acute lack of belonging, he missed a peer group, perhaps they should have made more effort getting him into a school, but he'd have been even more the odd one out, his accent wouldn't have helped much in finding friends amongst what Norman called, in a rather superior way, 'country bumpkins.' How much had he belonged in his own home, anyway? Robert didn't know whether he'd contacted any of his friends since he'd been here, the kids he played with all seemed to live in the same street. It had been like that in the Bronx, a kind of bounded place, a series of territories demarcated by a couple of blocks, where you knew what sort of kid he'd be if he came from 22nd and River Street or from 9th and Belingham. He guessed Keith would like to be with Alfie and the rest now, even with the sirens and sitting in garden shelters; he'd seen a photo of one, it looked claustrophobic and pretty ineffective if an explosive dropped nearby.

There was an opening in front of him; he must have reached the gate. He stepped up from his trail and went towards it. The sky was clear, stars patterning the dark. He looked both ways along the lane and was about to carry on along the next stretch of his path when he saw what looked like a handkerchief on the grass. He picked it up, wondering whether it belonged to Prudence until he saw an embroidered 'K' on a corner of it.

He looked around him, unsure of what he was looking for or what he expected to see. He had no idea, if it did belong to the boy, why it should be here or how long it had been. He shouted Keith's name again feeling it was even more pointless. He looked at the handkerchief, this time noticing a smear of dried blood near the opposite corner to the initial. Quelling a panic he tried to think. This, according to Doug, was where the man had found Prudence; perhaps it was his and he'd placed it on her face when he put his jacket over her, or it could have belonged to a friend of hers and she happened to have it with her and had come to and, feeling blood on her face, used it to wipe it off. He began more haphazard explanations to stop him thinking it was Keith's and what could have happened to him.

He had to stop running because he was out of breath, but he liked walking in the dark anyway, well, sometimes. He didn't like being in the farm fields, it was lonely and he could go quite a way before he saw any lights. He'd laid down in the middle of the back field once and the only lights he'd seen were the stars. Here, there were streetlights lighting up the buildings and shops and walls. He went down a side turning and stretched up over a privet hedge to see in a lit window a woman laying a baby on a sofa and covering it with a lacy shawl. She then picked it up and started feeding it. He wanted to be the baby, though didn't think he'd much liked being one. There was a memory he wasn't sure of, it was about nipples, he didn't feel he'd enjoyed them; they'd tasted bitter and wouldn't stay in his mouth. And he thought he remembered when he was hungry sometimes and his nappy being taken off, though he hadn't done anything in it, and a fresh one put on, but he wasn't fed. He also had a memory of dad shouting in the back room one night while he was standing up in his cot crying. He felt a bit like crying now. He wasn't going to though, he was a big boy. He supposed Lenny slept in his old room now; he couldn't stay in mum and dad's room for ever.

Returning to the main road he thought he saw a Dereham bus, but it was going the other way, back past the station. He didn't think there were any bombing raids here, the people who lived here were lucky, they didn't have to sit in an iron cave and feel it move when bombs dropped nearby nor have to put fingers in their ears to stop the sound. A bomb wasn't just a big bang, sometimes it was a smashing, splitting sound that roared and growled for minutes afterwards.

CHAPTER EIGHT

He wasn't really sure which way Ripton was, but needed to ask somebody because he had to get there, had to see whether Prudence was lying in the cold. He went up to a man looking in a shop window at some toys and games; perhaps it was his son's birthday tomorrow and he was thinking of buying him a present; dad probably did that, unless he got it cheap from the warehouse or bought it second hand. He asked the man.

'It's that way,' he said, pointing. 'There's no buses now I don't think. You wanna Dereham one, o' course. You on yer own?'

He turned and ran again; he didn't want the man calling a policeman because he might have to tell him what he'd done.

'Hey, bor.' he heard the man shout and as he turned into an alley wondered why people called him 'bor.' He came into a road parallel with the one he'd left and walked quickly along it. He wished Alfie was here; perhaps he'd been evacuated by now, but he would have gone to Essex. He should write to him, he supposed, he hadn't really thought about it. He probably wouldn't be interested in reading anything about farms and cows though, and he couldn't tell him about the black lady, he'd have written back and told him to go to the police. Alfie would never go to the police, not since he'd punched in a window of the public baths opposite where the big bomb had dropped and somebody had reported him. A policeman had gone to his house and told his parents, but he never admitted doing it. Keith hadn't seen a policeman since he'd been here; perhaps they didn't have any.

The front gardens were bigger here than at home, but they had the same sort of hedges. Doris Hill's dad used to shape a dog's head on his which everybody thought was silly, but it was clever the way he did it. He liked Doris; she was fat, but intelligent. He liked Pauline Porter who lived next door but one to Alfie best. He'd asked her to go to the park with him once, but his mother and Aunt Flo were there. He'd never seen mum in the park before and they'd come across and spoken to them with aunt Flo looking at him and Pauline, grinning all the time and nudging mum with her elbow. He'd felt embarrassed and, somehow, guilty and he and Pauline went back to their road and he'd never asked her again.

There were less shops and offices, but more houses now, though he did pass a cafe he'd have liked to have had a cup of tea in, but it was closed. He'd heard Mister Robert explaining the importance of cafes to Jess. They were places of 'succour and comfort, would-be breasts.' Mum always called breasts, 'bosums.' People in cafes were, he'd said, 'gulping at the nipple.' He wasn't sure why he remembered him saying it, but he said lots of interesting things like that. He talked to Norman about a man named Freud who said we were all lazy and pleasure seeking. Dad would have agreed with him, he didn't seem to like pleasure except having a drink and a smoke. He looked a bit grumpy when people were enjoying themselves, like when mum and aunt Flo danced together in the parlour listening to the wireless which was on loud in the back room and he came in from work and caught them; they looked a bit embarrassed. It was like a teacher coming into a classroom and catching boys playing about. He never took him to the pictures like mum did, but he did buy him a second hand Scalectrix figure-of-eight with model cars on it, but he didn't really care about cars, he'd have preferred a water colour paint box and some pointed brushes. He would have liked to have painted a picture now of the trees in the front gardens, but he didn't know how to paint the night, the black wasn't dark enough in water colours. Maybe he could write something about it, but didn't know what to say except about the light from the moon falling on the roof tops and chimneys. There were more trees at the side of the road now and he thought he heard an owl and perhaps a fox; he'd first heard them on the farm, he'd never seen any in West Ham.

The road was a bit narrower and the street lights more spread out. Perhaps he was going as far as his sewer walks or when he went over the Flats. He would go through the park, up Upton Lane past the 'Thatched House' pub and the station and then run across the grass and around the lake and the gorse bushes. Near the other end of the Flats was a black 'City of London Corporation' sign that he'd scratched a penis and testicles on with his penknife. He'd done big balls, but a small penis because when he'd been in the Chase near aunt Gwen's he'd seen a man do a wee behind a tree and when he shook his willie it was big and it frightened him.

He kept walking, the stars seemed brighter now and the sky in front of him was lighter, because, he supposed, it was above Dereham. He heard a car behind and saw his shadow flung in front of him and pushed himself into a hedge. Norman had told him always to walk on the side of the oncoming traffic. He crossed the road and looked across the fields, you couldn't tell what colour they were, it was too dark, but some were slightly different from others, he could tell those that had been ploughed from those with

CHAPTER EIGHT

something growing on them and make out the shapes of trees. There didn't seem to be any buildings where he was now, it was all flat and went on for miles. He wanted to write something about it, but couldn't think of what to say again, 'dark ditches, black bushes' he thought of, but knew it was too ordinary, 'haloed horizons' seemed to be better. But, he didn't care; he was cold and wanted to be with mum and Lenny. Mum used to say interesting things too, like, 'To a woman love is everything, to a man it's a thing apart,' and like dad saying that Mrs. Bowhay was 'up the duff again.' He supposed it meant that she liked plum pudding for her afters. He didn't understand these sayings, he thought, because he wasn't grown up enough. He stopped again. He knew he could still go back to the station and wait for the first train of the morning, it would be warmer there and maybe the buffet opened early, he still had some money with him.

He heard the tractor before its lights lit up the side of the field, he could tell by the sound what it was, it reminded him of when he'd looked up out the shelter and heard the noise of a German bomber he'd seen caught in criss-cross searchlight beams with puffs of smoke called 'flak' around it, but it wasn't hit. The sound got louder then suddenly quieter. He didn't look behind him.

'You alright, bor? Goin' anywhere?'

He turned; it was a big, new one. The man had a cap on like dad wore and blue overalls. 'You lost?'

'No.' His voice sounded like a squeak.

'You wanna lift somewhere then?' Where you goin'?'

'Norman's farm.'

'Don't never 'ear o' that one.'

'Heath Park it's called.'

'Oh, Heath, I'm just past there, ol' man Cleaver 'ad that, 'is son's got it now, over in France I 'eard, bet he's 'avin' fun there. I'll take you there. Jump on the back o' the trailer there, you'll 'ave to move a few things. My name's Peter Bovey.'

He went around the back, pulled himself up, slid a spade, pickaxe and fence post along the wooden floor to make room and sat with his legs dangling out the back. It was a bit bumpy, but better than walking and he could see the sky behind him lit now by the lights of Norwich. It was a bigger and noisier machine than Doug's. He liked dangling his legs, it was like being on a swing or roundabout, but not the one that used to come down his street on a cart that was tipped at an angle and which he once fell off. A lorry came up behind them and hooted and the tractor had to move almost into a field to let it pass.

'You not that evacuee Doug was talking of, are yer? You play with 'is boy sometimes.'

'Yes.' He had to shout so Peter Bovey could hear him.

'You're from London I suppose, what's it like there?'

He didn't know how to answer.

'They been gettin' a whackin' there an't they, s'ppose that's why you're 'ere. I'll go on round and drop yer off at your drive.'

He didn't want that, he wanted to stop at the gate. He asked if he could be dropped off at the back field.

'Where the sign is? We're almost there now.'

The tractor stopped a few yards before the gate. He jumped off.

'Thank you.'

'Pleasure. Mind you get in quick.'

He waited till the man drove off then went to the gate. He stood on its bottom rail and looked over the top of it. He couldn't see her, but saw a light where the old stream went under the trees then a man holding a torch walking across and picking something up near the tree where she fell. It was Mister Robert.

The relief flooding into him was followed by anger.

'Where the hell you been? Watcha doin' here?' Academia gone, the return of the Bronx. 'How long you been here?'

Keith stayed on the gate, unmoving, his eyes shut, protecting them from the torchlight. Robert held it down and walked to the side of the gate, unlatched it and swung it towards him, Keith still standing on it.

'Are you gonna get off or play games?'

He stepped down and stood there.

'Move then, move yourself, I want to shut it.' He could hear himself shouting.

He held the handkerchief up. 'Is this yours? It has your initial.'

Keith was silent.

'What's it doing here?' he yelled again. He gave him time to answer; when it came it was barely audible.

'I put it on the lady's face when she fell down.'

'When did she?'

CHAPTER EIGHT

'After you argued with her.' The voice was a little firmer. There was no point in asking what he'd been doing here; he'd seen them.

'She just fell?' Another wait.

'I pushed her and she fell over. I put it on her face, it was bleeding.'

'You pushed her? Why? Why didn't you come after me and tell me?' He heard his 'Why's' like clumps of percussion echoing around the field.

'I didn't mean to hurt her, honest, she seemed... bad.'

He stifled his next question; it had obviously upset him to see them arguing, he was possibly scared, too. It occurred to Robert that he may have never seen an African or black person before.

'Where have you been all day?'

He was told about the bus, station, the tractor. 'Is she alright now?'

'She's in hospital, but getting better. I'm glad you came back. I think we should go see her tomorrow. You should tell her you're sorry.'

'Should I take some flowers?'

'Yes, let's go back, go to bed.'

'Why do you know her Mister Robert?'

'She's a student.'

He rested a hand on Keith's shoulder imagining him gently laying his handkerchief on the side of her face; it was thoughtful, caring. They made their way back to the house. It was in darkness.

After he'd made supper, which they ate silently, though his anger was draining away, he sent Keith to his room then went up himself a little later and tucked him in; it was pleasant to do so and Keith seemed comforted. He went towards the door.

'Why is Prudence's skin so dark?'

He turned back to him. 'Well, it's a bit late for a biology lesson, but it began about a million years ago I think, when light-skinned people moved from rain forests to very hot areas and started losing their hair, so darker skin pigment was produced by the body to stop this which also helped to protect them from the ultra violet light of the sun; it's called Evolution. You know as much as I do now. Goodnight.'

He slept in patches, the underlying relief that the boy was safe in bed and Prudence apparently recuperating in hospital was disrupted by thoughts of going to see her in the morning and facing her, though aware that it would be worse for the boy.

He fried eggs sunny side up for breakfast, exaggerating his indigenous accent to tell a few childhood jokes while Keith sang bits of War songs he'd heard then both got ready for the drive to Norwich.

It wasn't a large hospital nor very busy. He bought some flowers at its entrance, told someone of the person he'd come to see and was directed to the fifth floor and asked to wait outside the ward. He suggested Keith rehearse what he was going to say to her, but be honest; he would go in first then come out for him. He handed him the last of his Hershey bars to keep him company.

It was a small ward with only four beds, one had a patient who was asleep; the others were unoccupied except for hers. She was sitting up, reading; a small plaster on her cheek, somehow, like a scar, making the rest of her face seem more beautiful. He walked towards her. She laid her book on the bed cover and frowned.

'Do you know what happened? Have you seen the boy?'

'Yes, he's the one we're looking after, he's very sorry, he didn't mean to hurt you.'

'But he did. And you haven't looked after him that well, have you; I'm wearing a cast under this sheet. Why did he do it?'

'Because he heard you and me arguing, it upset him, he wasn't against you, he doesn't know you, but what you… represented.'

'What was that then?

'Look, you've got to accept this, okay it's my analysis only, but let's assume he hasn't seen a black person before; subconsciously, an instant reaction would be fear, not just because you look different, we're wired to react against something different, it's a survival thing, but maybe because -'

'He was that frightened? Kill or be killed?'

'You're being unfair.'

'I'm in pain.'

'I know, but you're too bright not to see some sort of logic in this, he's not twelve yet, a child, a damaged one at that; perhaps you resurrected a bad experience, who knows? He was confused, he ran away, I think he may have even intended to go back to his home in London.'

She was quiet, looking down. 'It's hard for me to accept that I could create that reaction.'

CHAPTER EIGHT

'He tried a grin. 'Quite, you're a woman; you're not supposed to be frightening.'

'What about witches?'

'You're too attractive to be a witch,'

'But mothers can be terrifying, cant they?'

'The hand that rocks the cradle rules the world?'

'What about the argument that man has the magic wand that rules the world?'

'Glad to see you're feeling better.'

She turned her head to look at the stacked pillows behind her and asked if he would remove a couple so she could lie back and rest. He did. She lay there silently staring at the ceiling. He asked her if she knew how long she would be here.

'Two more days, apparently. I hate hospitals, they're so neutral. I'm glad this one's here though.' She gestured towards the chair by the bed. 'You could sit down. How's the boy feeling,?'

'Pretty guilty. He's outside, I'll get him, leave you alone.'

'Coming back?'

'Of course.'

He knew he should say sorry, but while Mister Robert was in the room with her he wanted to get away from the hospital, but didn't know where to go. He didn't really want to see her again, Mister Robert could apologise for him. But, it was him that had hurt her and it was only right that he should say sorry, that's what mum would have said. He pictured her face all bandaged, with blood soaking through and the bed sheet covering only part of her so that her leg with a steel rod attached to it was showing; he didn't want her to be groaning or crying. A nurse passed him and smiled. He liked nurses; when he was in hospital with dysentery a little while before Lenny was born, one with blue eyes and black hair looked after him; she was Irish and he couldn't always understand what she was saying, but she used to rub his tummy sometimes. For a month he could only eat rice and semolina, which he sometimes had for afters at school, and M & B tablets from a factory in Dagenham he used to pass on the District line when he went with mum to aunt Gwen's. She was nicer than Doctor Murphy with his big red face and hands and who told mum that it was, 'only indigestion, mother,' when she took him to the surgery. But it hurt more than that and he used to sit in the lavatory outside sweating and holding his stomach. Once, uncle

Harry had banged on the door shouting, 'urry up, what yer doin' in there?' There was a girl in the next bed with diarrhoea who looked like Pauline Porter and he'd asked her to marry him when they were both better and grown up, but she'd left before him.

When Mister Robert came out and told him to go in he just sat there until he was pulled up and guided through the doors. He saw her right away; she was reaching down to some pillows on the floor. She was doing it a bit slowly so he went over, picked them up and gave them to her. She thanked him and asked him to put them behind her head while she bent forward. He placed them there and smoothed them with his hand. She thanked him again, leant back and told him to sit on the chair.

'Well?' she asked.

He gave her the flowers.

'Thank you.'

He was still a bit frightened and looked at her cheek.

'It's only a small cut and it won't leave a scar.'

He looked down at her leg under the sheet. She pulled the sheet up.

'Look, It's a plaster cast which holds my ankle steady for a little while till the bone heals, it's not actually broken and doesn't ache as much as it did. My headache's gone, too. Have you anything to say to me?'

He thought a while. 'I like the way you speak, it sounds nice.'

'And?'

'I'm sorry for pushing you; I didn't mean you to go to hospital.'

'Do you know why you did it?'

'No. I won't do it again.'

She laughed. 'Well, that's good to know.'

He looked at the plaster. It was so white. He asked her whether he could draw something on it if he did it very gently. She nodded. He took his pencil, leant towards her foot and turned his head to her. She nodded again and, picturing the sketch he'd done at the station, drew her eyes and made them as dark as he could without pressing hard and, just suggesting the tip of her nose, drew her lips, making them fuller than before and giving them a dark outline. He heard her say 'Ouch.' but it was said quietly and when he looked at her she was grinning.

'I can't see that properly from here, but it's me isn't it.'

CHAPTER EIGHT

He was pleased and didn't bother to draw the outline of her face because she knew it was her.

'Come here.' she said.

He walked around the side of the bed towards her and she hugged him. He could feel her shaking a little bit and also noticed his cheek getting wet. He started to cry, too, but remembering dad saying he had to be a brave soldier, stopped himself. Mister Robert came in then and told him to wait outside again. As he went out she said, 'You're a clever boy.'

She was wiping an eye as he went over to her and sat down.

'Made up then?'

'Yes. He did this.' She pointed to her foot.

'It's you, he got it.'

She looked quickly around the ward. 'Still don't want to see me any more outside class?'

He looked down, saying nothing.

'If you're not going to answer you may as well go.'

'I do want to see you; I have this crazy urge to take you home and look after you.'

'Pity?'

'More than that. Your father coming?'

'I haven't told him.'

'I've got to tell Norman, at least about Jess.'

'And me?'

'I guess so, and probably about this, too, it'll get around; even if it doesn't, he's responsible for the boy also.'

'Perhaps you should take him home now, I'll rest.'

'I'll come tomorrow; I've got a seminar, I'll leave early.'

'I know, I'm occasionally in it.'

He bent and kissed her forehead, trailing his hand along her shoulder and arm, and rejoined Keith.

It was too late to go back to the house; Norman's train would be here in a couple of hours, so he suggested they have something to eat in town before going to the station. It was Keith who spotted the Lyons' tea shop and asked if they could go there. It was the little round drum of vanilla ice ream he liked, especially peeling off its paper wrapping. He told Robert the waitresses were called nippies and Iris Miller and Doris Hill wanted to be ones when they grew up. Robert smiled occasionally while he listened and ate sponge fingers and drank tea, but was thinking of what to tell Norman. He tried to take an interest in the tea shop's vague mixture of art nouveau and the moderne of its interior, but the absence of Jess at the house and Prudence's presence in her ward bed were too prescient.

They stood at the ticket barrier, Robert wondering why railway stations seemed to hold this dramatic frisson as trains came and went, the latter perhaps symbolizing a sense of loss, of absences, temporary or permanent, the former of meetings, re-unions, the ending of a long wait. He watched Norman's train arrive, its engine rolling slowly towards the buffers, its smoke pushing upward and slowly drifting through the roof trusses, piston steam squirting across the platform. A woman in a green fox fur left a carriage, another in a shoulder padded jacket eagerly smiled at a man running towards her from behind the barrier; it was a kind of theatre. Norman appeared wearing a double breasted suit and holding a brief case, looking as much a fighter as if he'd been shadow boxing and wearing a robe; the Henry Armstrong of academia. He smiled and shook Robert's hand.

'How are you Keith?' he asked, rubbing the top of the boy's head. Robert asked him what his journey was like.

'Fine, except for the stereotypes in the carriage, they played roles in such excesses of cliché as to be embarrassing. The pencil-moustached man opposite me who was a rep, the woman-on-a-train-with-child, the latter depositing sticky hand marks and sweet wrappings over a large part of the interior and... you know, it's all a conspiracy to annoy me. How's Jess?'

'Do you want to go straight back?'

'Yes, there are some things I want to write up and I could do with a very English cup of tea.'

Not much was said on the journey, Norman talking a little of some research he'd done and the friend he'd stayed with, and Keith staring out the window.

After only a little to eat, Keith asked Robert to read to him before he went to bed and, while Norman was getting the supper, read some of 'Little Lord Fauntleroy,' a book he had brought with him when he first came there; a piece of working class wish fulfilment, as Norman would have phrased it.

He didn't know whether to begin his erstwhile confession before, during or after their meal, the decision being made for him as Norman sat down at the table and asked after Jess again. He ate

CHAPTER EIGHT

lustily while Robert, sometimes haltingly, attempted a précis version of what had happened. Norman put his utensils down on a half completed meal and shook his head.

'You can't sociologize your way out of this and talk of deviant acts like yours as culturally variable even if you were going to, you did wrong, Robert, wrong by Jess. It's bound to get around the university, it's all a bit messy and it'll come back on you. Let's hope what the boy did can be kept between the parties concerned, otherwise that also will eventually be blamed on you. I really don't want to moralize, but I don't think you'll be able to keep working there. My God, Robert, I was about to recommend to them that your position be made permanent, but now… ' He looked down at the table then up again. 'You probably have the same analysis as me: this place, the countryside, all new to him and he's probably never seen anyone but British before has he, probably not that, just English. I'm right aren't I. Poor kid, poor Mnedi.'

'I'm glad you're not seeing the boy's actions as a white equals good, black equals bad thing, though he could have picked up some of that from his background, especially his father.'

'Of course not, it has little to do with crude prejudice or ideology, it's more to do with the symbolizing of white as purity, cleansing and salvation, if you will, day versus night; we can't see in the dark, we're vulnerable, bad things can happen. This is deep within us, our primitive psyche. Admittedly this sounds a bit weighty in the context of a child pushing someone over, but she was hurt. His fear prevented him from perceiving her as a person; she was, for a second, perhaps, a thing, at least until he saw her lying there. She could have represented so many things in that instance, a bad birth experience even.'

'Maybe we can forget that now; they're both getting over it.'

'What about you, are you getting over it?' Jess'll come back will she not?'

'I don't know; she was pretty sore.'

'What sort of relationship do you have with him, d'you think you could be becoming a surrogate dad?'

'I haven't thought about it.'

'Perhaps it could be that he feels, though unable to recognize it completely, he doesn't belong to his parents and unconsciously he's looking for his real ones.' He looked across the table at his protege. 'I'm sorry Robert, I really haven't much choice, I'm disappointed, not just in the moral context, I sound like a priest here I know, but that you won't be at the university. You're generally liked there, the students like you, but it'll have to happen. I'm sorry. Oh, and to add to your troubles, though you may not be aware of it, a suburb of Norwich was hit last night, a stick of bombs, no one was killed; it's a good thing it was far enough away. It also happened a couple of weeks ago too, it was kept quiet apparently. Incidentally, you can stay here whatever you do, not much chance of getting back to the States is there, shipping, torpedoes, etcetera. I'm to bed now. Goodnight.' He left the room.

Robert's sleep was laced by fragmented dreams of teaching at a local Infants school trying to control kids who made fun of his accent, travelling like a gypsy handy man around East Anglian farms selling his carpentry skills, and black and white newsreel shots of unemployment queues back home.

In the morning it was Geography time for Keith, but he'd be left on his own for the afternoon till Norman was back from work when Robert would see Prudence again. He felt a slight, automatic reflex as he thought of the visit, as if he *should* go, an expectational norm based on social consideration and guilt, but it wasn't, he wanted to see her, sit beside her bed, listen to her intelligence, sarcasm, her sometimes surprising insights.

On his way to work after setting the boy some questions on the Balkan countries, trying to remember their names himself, he thought of Norman's question regarding him and Keith. He wondered if he was purposely attempting to create himself as a surrogate father, to compensate for the emotional vacancy between him and his real one. He became aware that he'd been seeking similarities between his own childhood and the boy's. Why was he? He tried to dig into himself. Perhaps the child in him wanted a soul mate and, from what he knew of the boy's background, he could be the one; be his friend, his ally. He could also want Keith to be a younger version of himself and be projecting that version onto him, a cardinal sin, Norman would say, in psychotherapy, it would get in the way of a professional relationship, in this case, a non-professional one, one which was suggestive of his own immaturity, of him being the needy one. Maybe he should look for dissimilarities, try to disprove his theory of himself; if you wanted evidence to confirm a theory that much, you'd find it. He did remember, though, Keith telling him of the hostility around him

CHAPTER EIGHT

sometimes when he'd spoken a word of three syllables or more, it had happened to himself when he was a kid and from Junior High to his father and Billy.

It was sunny; he caught a bus from the university to the hospital, getting off a stop before. There was still a slight sense of surreality that he was in this place, in this part of the world, going where he was going, looking at the buildings, trees, the vehicles moving on the wrong side of the road and thinking of the woman he was about to see and the one who wouldn't be there when he returned to where he was living and that, when his temporary contract ended in a few weeks, he would no longer have a job.

Getting off the bus as the road bent towards the hospital, noticing a Gothic residue in the design of the gables and the arch above the main entrance, he heard a sudden droning and looked up. A two-engine aircraft, a dark shape against the blue sky, was climbing away from the building. He stopped and watched it go higher, then the sound seemed to smash his eardrums. A belch of flame and smoke erupted from the roof, bricks, slates and shattered lumps of concrete and glass flew away from the far end, smashing and crunching onto the road below. For a moment he couldn't relate cause and effect: the airplane, which he could still see, and the explosion. People began to run, some shouting or screaming. An old man was crouched on the pavement, his arms raised above his head, while a woman was helped to her feet by two men and pushed into a doorway to escape from the hail of debris from the upper floor where floorboards had slid out from a gaping corner, the ends of them vibrating. A trolley, filing cabinets, trays of surgical instruments glinting in the sun, sheets of paper like a flock of birds fell and a falling window with curtains wrapped around it smashed through the roof of a parked car.

Pushing his shock away he ran across to the old man and led him into the doorway of an adjacent building then looked around to see if there was anything he could do; people seemed to be either huddled in doorways or standing on the opposite side of the road looking up, either at the smoking upper floor or the vanishing aircraft. Prudence. She was on the fifth floor, one below the top. He pictured her, flung out of her bed by the violent rush of air, lying crunched against the bottom of a plaster-less wall, her face burnt. He ran to the entrance and through the doors seeing no one, there was hardly a sound. He heard the clanging of fire engines in the distance as he ran up the stairs, passing some nurses. There was a swirl of dust on the landings, more on the stairs as he went higher and cracked panes of glass in the doors of the ward he wanted. He pushed in and saw, dropped at an angle from the far corner of its ceiling, the end of a girder resting in the middle of a bed, her bed, the mattress risen from the bedsprings curling around the red painted shaft of steel. He stared at the two neat, windowless gaps beneath its other end held up by a wooden ceiling joist as plaster and brick dust fell and blew about him.

'What are you doing here?' The voice came from behind him. 'Get out, come down.' It was a nurse, a Sister.

'There was… there was a patient in that bed.'

'I think she's in the canteen; everybody's to go to the basement now. Come on.' She turned away; he followed her down the stairs. Nurses, doctors, other medical staff and those patients who were fit enough were coming out of ward doors and hurrying down the stairs to the basement, a few on the ground floor carrying bits of meals they'd been eating in the canteen. As he went behind her into the basement she said, 'You can help.'

He saw her almost immediately, pressing a young girl against her good leg, stroking her hair. He moved around people towards her in the quickly filling area. She looked at him. 'I'm okay, help that lady over there.' She pointed to an elderly woman trying to get up from the floor, her arm in a sling. He hesitated then helped her gently up and looked for some chairs, there was an empty one by an open door marked 'Boiler Room.' He led her there, sat her down and, seeing some cups on a table near one of the boilers, got some water from a wall tap and brought it out to her. Bedding and chairs were carried in, nurses were tending shocked patients, a few were crying, a doctor was injecting a young woman with something. Two firemen came in asking if everyone was alright and before anyone could answer the basement doors swung open and an authoritative voice said loudly, 'Everyone alright? It seems to be okay now, it was only the one aircraft, it may have wandered off course, who knows, but there's no enemy plane anywhere near here now; let's be thankful the top floor was being used mainly for storage. I hope it won't affect your treatment and recuperation too much.'

The man went out again, stethoscope swaying across his white coat. As the air cleared, a kind of ordinary silence took over, his words seeming to have had the effect almost of turning the attack into a merely unwanted interruption.

CHAPTER EIGHT

Robert looked around him, there wasn't much more he felt he could do. People were being settled down, someone announced that the canteen was still functioning and asked for volunteers to help bring tea and cakes down from it and a nurse was taking the young girl from Prudence; she looked a little sad to be losing her. He went across to her and put his arms around her, at first gently then harder, he was hurting her. He pulled away; she wiped her tears and forced a grin.

'It was horrible, I was in the canteen, it was the first time I'd been out of bed. I was helped to the lift, I'd just begun to eat and then the noise. It was… ' She shook her head. 'Were you coming to see me?'

'Of course.'

'Thanks.'

'Don't thank me.' He was about to mention the girder on her bed, but decided not to. 'Your ward's in a mess, guess they'll put you in another one. How's the leg?'

'Getting better, perhaps they'll send me home today, make space for someone else.'

'Does your father know where you are?'

'No, but I shall tell him, he's bound to find out about the bomb. He'll probably get me into a clinic in London.'

'Why?'

'Don't you want me to leave here?'

'No, I don't want you to go anywhere.'

The Sister who had spoken to him came up to them and said slowly and deliberately, 'Miss Mnedi, we'll get your belongings from the ward and put you on another floor. Come.'

She took her elbow and guided her away. Her patient looked back at him as they reached the door and resignedly shrugged.

He took a bus back to the university, the passengers talking amongst themselves about what had just happened and seeming rather bewildered. He had only one class and would tell Keith when he returned that it was only a small bomb and that Prudence was alright. He thought of the black and white Robert Doisneau photographs on a wall at the French café in Barons Court he'd sat in: a couple kissing on a street corner, a pavement accordionist, a man leaning over to watch a street artist, his dog staring mournfully at the camera, and wished their memorable resolutions could be applied to his own life.

CHAPTER 9

He was angry at the world. The shock of the bomb the previous day was withdrawing and he was reacting to it, that and his own sense of foreboding. He was teaching. One of his students had mentioned the 'rock bottom' explanations of psychology. He laughed.

'Where do you think it all comes from then? All in the genes is it? Is this the 'state of technology' argument; that one day scientists will discover where all our behaviour, social responses too, comes from? Will they find a gene that has, 'Little boys pinch green apples.' printed on it? Our behaviour, feelings, of pride, fear of punishment, of guilt, it's all learnt. Have we not agreed on this? He was gesticulating, emphasising. 'As children, we're told that we musn't do something, that it's bad manners, mum tells us and whatever we're told becomes as near to a guiding absolute as you'll get. You English talk of someone as 'common.' meaning low down the social hierarchy, the way they speak, act, it's the same virtually everywhere in the world and, yeh, it's tribal, of course, our feelings are largely moulded and reinforced socially by non-codified laws, norms, sanctions. Your mother didn't pick these things out of the air to fling at us, it's inside her, she got it from the world around her, the world of values, of what's perceived as right and wrong, good and bad, correct or incorrect, all backed up not only by significant others but... It's primary and secondary socialization and it's passed on ad infinitum, you know this, anyway.'

'You're coming down on the side of society makes man aren't you, the blank slate.' asked the student he'd initially responded to.

'Yes I am.'

'What about love?' someone asked.

'A reification.' He imagined Prudence's face in front of him smiling and saying, 'And look how real *that* feels.'

'Look, I don't think we can really mix and match here, we can't just pick bits of behaviour and say that's genetic, that's deeply psychological or that's culturally learnt behaviour, though I'm more for the latter of course. It's a mess. Maybe we should have some sort of meta-narrative here, one or the other as a prerequisite for a generic understanding of behaviour. Okay, it lacks shades of grey but... ' He

CHAPTER NINE

shrugged. 'Maybe we can use this as the topic of the final essay of this term; call it, 'Psycho versus Socio.' and go where it takes you.' He could see Prudence again, this time asking what the blank slate was made of. He knew it was the last essay he would set them.

In the evening he was able to go to the hospital because Norman would be with the boy again. He had, of course, heard about the bomb, but not where it had landed. When he was told what had happened he was a little shocked and gave Robert a hug. 'I know the English aren't supposed to do this sort of thing, but I'm relieved, I'm glad you're here.'

There was a fire engine at the corner of the building, council workers were still clearing rubbish from gutters and pavements and he could see workmen on the roof. A nurse told him that Prudence had been moved to a ward on the first floor. Again she was in a corner bed, but this time not alone, her father was with her, sitting listening to her, nodding earnestly. Robert paused, not quite sure what to do. She saw him and gestured for him to come over. Her father turned and stood, and rather cautiously shook his hand.

'How are you?' he asked in his baritone voice, 'My daughter has told me what happened. I am glad you were here.'

'Refer to me by my name, daddy, please, Robert does know it.'

'Yes. I see a chair over there, why don't you get it.'

He did. She put her fingers on the back of his hand as he leaned over and kissed her forehead, it seemed the thing to do, both men sharing a proprietary interest in her.

'They said I could leave tomorrow afternoon, but my father's going to take me away to London.'

He turned his face to Robert. 'We, the Embassy, have a clinic nearby that we use, I'm not mistrusting the expertise on offer here, but I want her near me for a while.'

She looked at Robert, raising her eyebrows. 'He's my boss.'

'Yes, my daughter, I am.' He looked at both of them with narrowing eyes. 'I will leave you alone for a little time.'

'The canteen's on the ground floor if you -'

'I passed a restaurant in the taxi. I shall eat there.' He patted her hand and left.

'How long has he been here?'

'A half hour or so. He heard on the wireless what happened and came right away. Heard from your wife again? Forget that, I won't ask about her any more, you tell me if you want to.'

'I haven't. I know this is a bit pragmatic, but are you up to date with the work you missed? You've come so far, pity to throw it away with the end in sight. Norman thinks you deserve an honorary degree.'

She grinned. 'People have been, and are, going through a lot worse. How's the boy?'

'Feeling better, I think you charmed him.'

'I just wanted to be honest with him.'

'And he, you.'

He heard footsteps approaching. 'I need to talk to my daughter again; I want to spend some time with her now.'

'That was a quick meal, Mister Mnedi.'

'Thanks for coming; I don't know whether I shall see you again.'

'You will, daddy, you will,' she said.

He held his hand out. Robert shook it then put his fingers to his lips, bent his palm towards her and left, feeing he'd been checked, prohibited, like a boy at school.

Keith hadn't really wanted to leave the lady at the hospital; he'd wanted to sit on her bed till the nurses told him to go. He would have liked to have laid next to her and looked at her face, her skin was so smooth. He was getting used to her hair now and couldn't imagine it not sticking up. He'd noticed a gold earring like a hoop on the table beside her bed; He supposed it was hers and that she'd wear it when she felt better. She'd said he was forgiven. He liked that better than at church and school assembly when the vicar or the Headmaster said that God forgave their sins, and in the prayer they'd had to learn about being forgiven their trespasses. Mum would say that she had a kind heart. He would like his mother to meet her. She'd be surprised first of all, but then she'd probably say to aunt Flo, 'Ooh, she has a lovely skin and there's something about her that's sort of posh, you wouldn't expect it would you, it's hard to explain, but she's so nice.' She wouldn't say anything to dad.

He missed Jess though, but didn't want to ask Mister Robert about her because he didn't think he wanted to talk about it; perhaps he'd done something wrong or she had and had gone away. He liked her cooking more than his and Norman's. She didn't like tomato sauce either, unlike his mum and dad, and had said to him, 'All sauces are stronger tasting than the food they are put on, therefore the food becomes nothing more than a texture for the sauce.' He wondered

CHAPTER NINE

whether she'd read it somewhere, his mother wouldn't have said it like that. Perhaps Lenny was having food like bacon and chips with sauce. He hoped he wasn't.

He was surprised when Jamie had told him Norwich had copped it. He didn't think bombs dropped in the country, but it was a city so there were more places to hit, like factories and houses, perhaps Mr. Colman's factory was a target. He didn't know why there was a war, perhaps nobody did really, it just sort of happened and people couldn't stop it, but maybe England had done something wrong and Germany was punishing them. Or it could be the other way round and what Germany was doing was wrong. He hadn't heard from mum for a while, he'd ask if he could ring her.

Two days later, a time marked heavily by the absence of both Jess and Prudence, though the latter had made a quick phone call giving him the address of the London clinic, Norman brought in an envelope for Robert that he'd picked out of the post box at the side of the main gate as he returned to the house. Recognising the writing he took it to his room and opened it. The preamble of his name was absent.

'I want to go home, but can't yet, this horrible war. I've found an office job - you know me - in London, near the area we first looked around, well, not far away. I'll be going there soon. I'll be okay; some say the bombing will be over pretty soon. It's at an Infants school and I'll be helping out in the classroom; it's not home, but I shall enjoy doing it, it'll be great with the younger kids. When this is over maybe I'll do it back home if I can. I miss you, but can't forgive you. I actually miss you less and less, Rob. Sorry. You need someone different from me. I've realised it for quite a while, but kind of not accepted it. Maybe you really *do* need someone like Prudence.
Say hello to Norman and give my love to Keith.
Jess.'

There was a quiet, almost casual finality about it. He re-read it. It seemed just as final. He felt as if he'd been kicked in slow motion by a horse. He wondered what he would do. He looked out of the long room window and past the end of the drive to the sloping hill and its copse of trees almost hiding the small quarry from which the stone that built the house had been excavated. He glanced along the road in front where, at the crossroads, it turned towards Ripton and its thatched cottages and Victorian pubs and houses. The feel of the place was small and ordered, but he was getting used to it, accustomed to its particular monochromes of green and brown, the cumulus that was rarely absent from skies greyer than at home, and the cows, the domestic ungulates as Norman referred to them, moving quietly around with the occasional sheep or two giving way to their lumbering progress. But he could surely only stay if he got a job locally, he couldn't expect Norman to subsidise him. He thought of London; he was raised in a city larger than this, amongst similar busy, noisy spaces, travelling on buses and screeching, grinding trains, looking across a river, and squashed into crowds between concrete constructions. He felt the familiar rhythms of a metropolis and along with it the feeling that this had been a kind of sojourn, a rural interlude, a working one, a stimulating one, but not permanent, and without the excitations and satisfactions of his job he wanted the city again. Just then the phone in the hall rang and a short while later Norman shouted up that Keith's mother wanted to speak to him.

He went down and listened to her. She hoped they were all well, but she'd heard about a Norwich hospital being bombed and thought, perhaps, that her son should come home. He heard someone in the background and a different, rather aspirational voice said into the phone, 'This is Gwendoline, Ruth's sister. The bombing seems to have stopped here now, we haven't had anything for days, perhaps there won't be any more and Ruth and I think he should come back.'

He couldn't really argue with this, it seemed rather ludicrous that someone should stay in a place where there were bombs and not return to their home where there were none.

'It's Mrs. Clements now; I think it's for the best.'

He told her they would have her son ready for her in a couple of days.

'Thank you, Mister Costain. Nice to have spoken to you I'm sure.'

He went into the kitchen where Norman was preparing a meal for them.

'Did I hear what I thought I heard?'

'Afraid so.'

'Why that reaction?'

'Because I'll miss him.'

'Well, at this moment I guess you will.'

'I don't think I could quite live for my job or, rather, profession as you seem to, though I think I'd like to.'

CHAPTER NINE

'Well, there are other things.' He looked up from peeling potatoes, 'I hope you haven't lost your other things.'

'You may have guessed who the letter was from. She's going to London soon to work. It seems she doesn't want to know me anymore.'

'That's for now, but -'

'I don't think it's just for now.'

The kitchen door opened and Keith came in from Jamie's. Robert told him to ring his mother at his aunt Gwen's and that their meal would be ready soon.

'Look, I don't know whether you're planning to find something around here but, other than this steak which is now going into the pan, this may be good news. I've heard that there could be an opening at a polytechnic in London, east London, a relatively new place and it's straight sociology I believe, which I feel would perhaps suit you rather more than what you're doing here; I think you feel that it's a bit of a theoretical confusion, am I right?'

'I hope I haven't made it too obvious.'

'Only a little bit, you're intellectually flexible enough, I think, to veer one way then the other in our discipline, knowing, like so much theory, it's an unanswerable chicken and egg thing, anyway. It's so easy to use a theoretical framework as a crutch isn't it, in fact more than one simultaneously, like Marx and Freud's opposing models. I'll contact the fellow who told me and get details from him and the rest is up to you. I'll obviously give you a good reference, take that as said.' He gave a rare grin. 'Maybe you could keep an eye on the boy there, eh?'

Robert went into the hall. Keith wasn't there so he went upstairs.

It was nice to speak to his mother again, but she sounded worried, she often did, really, and he could see her face looking anxious as she spoke. It seemed to worry her that it was a hospital that had been hit. Aunt Gwen spoke to him, asking what he'd been doing on the farm then said that the raids on London had stopped and they wanted him home. He asked if Alfie still had the wooden leg, but she didn't know. She put mum back on and she told him that Mister Robert had said he'd be home the day after next and that it was the best thing to do.

He went up to his room, closed the door and sat down on the floor behind it. He didn't know whether he wanted to go home or not. It seemed as if half his head and body wanted to and half not. He wanted to be with Mister Robert and Jess, but she wasn't here and he hadn't been told where she was. Perhaps he could be taken to America one day and Jess would be there and he could see her and the skyscrapers. He was doing a drawing for Mister Robert as a surprise, but it was taking a long while and when he wasn't drawing it he hid it under his bed. Also he'd just got to know Prudence and wanted to see her again. He sort of liked Norman, but didn't really care about not seeing the cows or sheep again; he couldn't really see the point of them. Jamie was alright he supposed, though he kept calling him 'Keefie' like Frankie Nutt did, but he hadn't done much with him that he'd wanted to, like play knock down ginger or tin can Tommy, but it would be difficult to play them here and there were only the two of them anyway; but he just might pinch one of his uncle's rabbit snares to serve him right. Jamie had come up with him on the roof that was like a turret where they'd pretended they were firing arrows at the Normans in the invasion. He'd made a bow out of a branch of the old elm tree in the front meadow and had shot a cane with a bit of Plasticine on the end at a bird pecking in the vegetable garden below and hit its back; he'd felt a bit sick after he did it.

He liked looking at the countryside more than when he'd first come here, it didn't seem quite so big now and some of it looked beautiful when the sun shone, but the sky was big and sometimes it made him feel small, especially at night. It was quiet here, too, and he wasn't sure if it wouldn't be too noisy for him in his road again with all the people that lived there and kids shouting, though he knew them anyway, and some were his friends. It smelt nice here, even the stink of the fresh cowpats he'd got used to, almost, and the birds always seemed to be calling and singing. Uncle Reg, who called London 'the smoke,' used to say, 'I love wakin' up in the mornin' and 'earin' the birds coughin'.'

There was a lot more space indoors here, the rooms weren't big, but there were more of them and the hall and landing were huge. The house at home seemed a bit squashed as he pictured it, and there would be six of them living in it now. He thought he wanted to play street games again, but wondered if he'd grown up a bit and would be a bit too old for them, he wasn't sure. He didn't want to stand outside any pubs again though.

CHAPTER NINE

There was a knock on his door and he felt himself pushed along the floor as it opened. It was Mister Robert. He asked him what he was doing down there. He stood up and told him that he'd been thinking abut going home. He was asked what he felt about it. He wasn't sure, but he knew that he had to go. He asked if they would see Prudence again.

'I hope so; she's going to a clinic in London.'

'Can I go with you when you see her?'

'I was going to see her after I'd taken you home to your mum, but I suppose, if you don't mind arriving a bit late, you could come with me. I haven't told your mother yet what time she'll see you.'

He asked if she would be at the station waiting for him.

'If you want, I guess, or I could take you there, depends on what your mum says.'

He told him that he'd like to see Prudence and then be taken back.

Next day he went to see Jamie and Doug to say goodbye. Doug shook his hand and Jamie, looking a bit sad, did too. Keith thought he was a bit young to shake hands, it was what adults did. As he couldn't play with Jamie because he was going into Norwich with his uncle, he walked across the fields to the back gate again which he'd nicknamed 'Prudence's gate.' Standing under the tree where he'd pushed her, he felt sorry again, but he was sort of glad he had because he'd seen her in the hospital and got to like her. Norman cooked a big meal for them in the evening and he thought that the steak was something else he'd miss and also the way Mister Robert put yoghurt and muscavado sugar on the porridge in the mornings. He liked the word, but thought it was too foreign and sort of dramatic to be just sugar. That night before he went to sleep he looked at the photo of Bluey on the mantelpiece in his room, which he'd forgotten to put in his case, and decided to leave it there to show he'd been here.

In the morning, when they got out of Norman's car at the station and he was given a hug by him, he told him that he looked like a boxer. Norman pulled some angry faces and pretended to punch him to make him laugh. He and Mister Robert didn't talk much on the train, though he was asked what he would miss most about the farm and what he thought would be the first thing he'd do when he got home. He couldn't think then he said he wanted to draw something on Bluey's shell.

The station where they changed trains for the Underground didn't seem as big as it had before, perhaps it was because he'd seen a few stations recently or else he'd grown a bit. He'd never been this far away from home on the Underground, mostly it had been with dad to Aldgate or, once, to Victoria, but this was South Kensington and there were lots of old buildings outside which Mister Robert, though hurrying, kept looking at in between studying a map.

The hospital building was probably only fifteen years old with some nouveau scrolls on the metal doors, a curved window here and there and lots of jade green and black inside the foyer which he would liked to have looked around, but instead asked the receptionist where he should go. Prudence's room was at the far end of the same floor. Robert had been oddly touched by Keith wanting to see her again, the feeling remaining with him as he'd helped him get his stuff ready for the journey: his clothes - Jess had bought him a jumper and a pair of shorts to add to his wardrobe - a few sheets of paper with writing or drawings on them and the gas mask which had stayed in its box till Robert had got it out for a look, Keith blanching as he did so; the feel, smell, the shape of it was, although having a potential usefulness, pretty repellent. He told him to wait for him on a bench outside the room while he went in and that he would come out for him like he did at the other hospital.

She was in a medical gown standing bent over the bed with her hands on the edge of it taking her weight.

'That's progress.'

'I'm assuming you would have been here earlier, but you've been looking at the buildings,' she said without looking at him.

'Thanks for the warmth of your greeting. Is the ankle less painful now?'

'Yes, I don't think I should be standing, but I want to be out of here.'

'I'd like you to be, too.'

'How's academia?'

'Well, in a short while I won't be observing it very closely, at least not at London University Anglia.'

'Why?'

'My contract's been terminated. I'm applying for a lecturing job on the other side of London.'

She sat on the side of the bed. 'What happened?'

CHAPTER NINE

'You did. But don't blame yourself. I had to tell Norman because my wife's gone and -'

'Have you heard from her?'

'Yeh, a letter, she's moving to London, I think it's over. The university would find out about your involvement and what happened to you, anyway. It's done with. What is it in the Rubaiyat? 'The moving finger writes and having writ moves on, nor all thy piety nor wit shall lure it back to cancel -''

'Don't get too literary, you're running away again. Do you blame me?'

'No, I've just said so. I don't think she's been happy for some time. Perhaps what you said at your place was right. Incidentally, the boy's outside, I'm on the way to take him back home to his parents and he wanted to see you.'

'That's nice; I'd like to see him.' She looked at him for a while and said, 'My period's late.'

'What does that mean?'

'Well, ordinarily, nothing, but I'm never late. Could be a hundred reasons, but... ' She gave him a grin that wasn't quite sure of itself.

'Are you saying that you could be pregnant or something?'

'Not 'something,' you either are or you aren't.'

His emotions suspended themselves. He heard the door open and the steel tips of her father's heels coming towards them. Ignoring Robert he stood at the other side of her bed and told her that he had a meeting to go to with the Ambassador and the Foreign Secretary's Africa Committee in Westminster.

'I'll be back to see you as soon as I can, probably in a few hours.' He turned to Robert. 'I'd like to see you for a moment.'

As he followed him out it was Robert this time who shrugged resignedly at Prudence. Outside the door her father raised a finger at him before Robert, seeing Keith sitting there looking up at them, suggested they mover further away. They went a few paces along the corridor.

'Who is the boy, anyway? Is he your son?'

'He is, was, an evacuee. I'm -'

'I know very little about you, you could be married, divorced, I don't know, but my daughter is obviously in some sort of relationship with you other than a teacher-student one, but she doesn't tell me everything. I don't know whether this sounds archaic to you, but I would like to know whether your intentions are honourable, I do not want her hurt.'

It did sound archaic, but not something to be taken lightly; he seemed a formidable man. Robert, thinking of the clichéd advice given when nervous of someone, to imagine them naked, tried to for a second then just as quickly changed his mind. Bracing himself, he said, 'Look, I know you love your daughter, I do, too, and I don't intend to hurt her, and yes, she's more than just a student, I was one once, only a little time ago for what it's worth. There's no need to get heavy with me.'

'Watcha gonna do, make me an offer I can't refuse?' he asked in an almost flawless Brooklyn accent. He grinned, his gold tooth shining. 'Well? Not bad for an African, eh?'

Robert smiled back; the unexpected moment was one full of feeling, of genuine warmth. The man laid his hand briefly on Robert's shoulder.

'We shall see each other again. This is an important meeting I am attending; perhaps I will be Ambassador one day.'

He walked quickly away, nodding at Keith as he passed, while Robert tried to accept what he had just said about Bheka Mnedi's daughter. He supposed it was true, true because he had spoken it unguarded, unintellectualized. He saw the boy looking perturbed and, still feeling emotionally discordant, told him to come into the room with him.

She was still sitting on the edge of the bed and gave Keith a big smile.

'Hello, young man. So you're going home then.'

'Was that your dad?'

'It was.'

'He has a loud voice and a shiny tooth.'

'Could you draw him?'

'I can remember his face, but don't know how to get the tooth colour.'

'Mix yellow with a bit of brown?'

'I'll do it when I get home.'

'I got a man to cut around your drawing on my plaster so I can put it up in my room in the embassy house.' She looked at Robert. 'I shan't be returning to the university, father rang Norman Lee who said that as I've almost completed my work, I don't have to. I do have one more essay to do, it's yours. 'Give examples of the

CHAPTER NINE

necessity of reification to society.' You've begged the question there, of course, but I'll forgive you.'

'It's just up your alley.'

'Yes, love is also a reified concept, is it not?'

'There's something I want to say to you.'

He was about to ask Keith to go outside again, but realising that the moment was inappropriate and, glancing at the wall clock above her bed aware that he'd be late getting him back, told her it was time to take the boy home. 'I'll stay somewhere tonight and come again tomorrow.'

'Make it early; I'll probably leave in the morning.'

He sat next to her on the bed. 'I could have sat here for the last fifteen minutes, couldn't I.' He put his arm round her shoulders, pulled her briefly to him and kissed her cheek.

'Will I see you again, auntie Prudence?' asked Keith

'Of course, Mister Robert will bring you, but not here, although I won't be far away. Give me a kiss.' He shyly did so.

They were both hungry and found a café in a nearby alley.

'My dad calls these, 'workmen's cafes,'' said Keith as they settled down to egg and bacon.

'Yeh, I guess we just have diners and bars.'

'Do you think you could take me to America one day, Mister Robert?'

Robert lazily imagined the boy in New York and thought of the effect on him of a foreign city three thousand miles away from his parents. It would be a cauldron of stimulus for his potential. Perhaps his aunt Gwen could help persuade them to let him go for a few months. They'd be in contact; phoning, writing. He could take him to Coney Island, the Empire State...

'More realistically, if I get this job, which wouldn't be far from you - they could well take me on for rarity value I guess, there's not many Americans over here, yet, anyway - I could live fairly near you maybe.'

'What, in the Portway? '

'That's at the top of your street, right? Shouldn't think so, but it won't be a million miles away.'

'I can see you then.'

'Yep, and in a few years, maybe, I could be teaching you. All the big words, Keith, uh?'

'Could we go to auntie Prudence's country?'

'Africa? Yeh, what's your geography like?'
'You should know Mister Robert, you taught me.'
'Don't be such a wise guy, buster.'
'Does she live in South Africa?'
'Southern Africa. Yeh, she'll travel backwards and forwards I guess, when the war's finished, that is. Maybe we'll get an invite when she goes there again, that'd be some trip, uh?'
'Do you like it here?'
'Well, I'm kinda getting used to it; I still think you're all drab and boring and say, 'please' and 'excuse me' all the time and your upper lip's too stiff and you're tight assed. Come on, let's get you home.'

Across the High road from Stratford station the town hall had sandbags copiously piled around its front and side and the ubiquitous crossed tape on its windows. Behind it was a brick shelter built at the side of the road and familiar gaps where shops and houses had been with the people passing by them hardly seeming to notice, as if it was the norm which, in some areas of the city, it was. They walked through the recreation ground, Keith telling Robert that if they had gone to Plaistow station he could have shown him the top of the sewer he used to walk along.

'And if we were in the Bronx, Keith, I coulda shown you where Billy and I used to sit in the Yankee Stadium and where the abandoned Subway station on the 6 line at Eighteenth Street is, but we ain't, are we.'

Keith thought that uncle Albert would have said something like, 'And if yer aunt 'ad bollocks she'd be yer uncle.'

As a cloud moved away from the late sun, the houses they were approaching were lit by it, their small bay windows glinting, chimney pots glowing red.

'See the chimney cowl on that house, the way it flashes as it goes around, a bit of magic, eh?'

'Why do you like buildings so much, Mister Robert?'

'It's the feel of the past, the pictures they conjure up I guess, maybe it's an escape or maybe I'm looking for a womb, Keith, a perfect one, perhaps we both are. I don't expect you to understand this, perhaps ever. Let's say they could be stopping me from feeling lost.'

CHAPTER NINE

'But I know where we are, when we go through the rec. gate we turn left into the Portway then it's the third turning on the right, number thirty eight.'

'Sure.'

Keith pointed to a house near the exit. 'Those bricks are called London stocks, they have names.'

'Bricks do? Like Billy Brick or Sid Cement?'

'That's silly. There's yellows and the red ones are called red rubbers. Do you like trees, too?'

'Sure, but they're wasted in the country; I mean, look at that one there almost framing that window, look at what it does to the bricks, it gives them a kind of magnificent shadow and... you're an artist, you understand.'

'Is it suppertime yet?'

'Maybe, why?'

'There's a fish and chip shop round the corner when we leave the rec. and I thought we could get some and take them home for my mum and dad, mum could put them in the larder for tomorrow if they've eaten already.'

'Fine, and perhaps we can have 'em if they don't, uh?'

They went to the shop, Robert watching he boy pulling a face when the meal was handed over accompanied by, 'Vinegar?' then went along the Portway, Keith sometimes seeming animated then slowing down so that Robert had to turn around till he caught up. He looked up and grinned at him.

'I can talk American, too. 'Okaaay, let's go baybeee.'

'Hey, everybody's doing it; I'm feeling more at home.'

'D'you think that black and white people would make black and white babies? Perhaps they'd be white with black spots or black with white stripes or -'

'Who's being silly now?'

'Do you like talking to Prudence?'

'Of course and I want to talk to her soon.'

'What about?'

'Something I need to say to her.'

'Is it good?'

'Guess it is, and that's an interesting looking church, let's get a little nearer, it's pretty old.'

'It's West Ham church.'

Robert crossed the road towards it walking quickly, with Keith hurrying to keep with him. They walked around the building, skirting the grave stones then out again at the far entrance.

'Was that good?'

'Yeh, we haven't got much like this stateside. Where do we go now?'

'You can get to it this way.'

They walked though an alley, an unusual one; narrow, but with tall Edwardian houses on one side of it. They passed another road, then, not needing Keith's cry of 'Here it is.' Robert followed him into his street. As they did so the boy asked him to stop for a minute and put his case - having refused Robert's offer at the station to carry it for him - on the pavement, opened it and pulled out a sheet of paper. He stood up and handed it to him. It was a detailed drawing of the top of the Chrysler Building, complete with glass wrapped corners and radiator cap gargoyles.

'It took me a long time to do.'

'Gee, I bet it did. Thanks very much, Keith, I shall treasure it. I'll have a good look at it tonight when I find somewhere to stay.'

'You could stay at my house.'

'Your mum hasn't the room, but it's okay.'

Robert asked if any of his friends were around.

'That's Frankie Nutt at the top; he's probably going over the park. We've just passed the Bowhays house, and Iris and Gwen live there and this is Doris Hill's.'

'Where does Alfie live?'

'Just over there, that's his mum in the porch with a hat on.'

Underneath a lamppost the tennis ball in the gutter was kicked vigorously away by Keith before saying, 'This is my house now, Mister Robert.'

'I know, and I think it's about time you stopped calling me 'Mister.''

'Okay, Mister... Okay, Robert.'

'You know, I think I'll keep an eye on you from time to time, maybe I'll even come and get sore with your maths teacher. Are you gonna knock then?'

'I want *you* to.'

As Robert lifted the knocker, Keith wondered if his brother had got any bigger.

EPILOGUE

Doris Hill did become a nippy, at a Lyons' tea shop in Aldgate; Iris didn't, being killed by a V-2 rocket while visiting a friend in East Han. Most of the Bowhay children joined the army, two dying on active service in the 'Forgotten War' in Malaya, Frankie Nutt and his mother moved to Billericay, while Alfie married Pauline which, even at 86, Keith, occasionally and maybe a little enviously, thinks of as bizarre. Ruth and Fred died at home in Elm Park, the former a year after her sister Gwen, and Flo and Harry's lives ended in Benfleet, Flo living till a hundred and two.

Jess, after her spell at a school in London, returned home before the end of the war doing similar work in the Bronx until retiring and living with her second husband and their adopted daughter. She and Robert never communicated with each other again except for their divorce, although for a time working in London only eight miles apart. Norman went to France and lived there till his death at seventy, Billy lived in the Bronx for the rest of his life next to the house he was born in and Bekha Mnedi became Ambassador for a short period before retiring to his farm. Robert lived in London and saw Prudence as much as he could between her prolonged visits near the war's end to Zulu Kwa Province where she did voluntary work. She had a miscarriage when involved in an accident in Knightsbridge in a car driven by her father's chauffeur, but never told Robert she was pregnant. He visited her on her father's farm on six occasions and returned to New York after the war where Prudence sometimes stayed with him. They never married and both died in the same year.

Keith also saw Robert and Prudence occasionally, before and after going to art school and becoming a commercial artist for a large advertising agency. He paid sporadic visits to a therapist for some years before attending university as a mature student then lectured in Art History at the same polytechnic as Robert did years before him, living in a sun trap house in a nearby conservation area that he often thinks Robert would have appreciated more than him. He married, had children and divorced twice. Lenny, after an unsuccessful engineering apprenticeship, did several jobs, including delivering soft drinks to West Ham football ground then, until his retirement, was a resident fireman at Buckingham Palace. Keith seemed to feel Robert's protective eye on him always and, strangely, still does.